Frances. Bevan

Hymns of Ter Steegen and Others

Frances. Bevan

Hymns of Ter Steegen and Others

ISBN/EAN: 9783337089757

Printed in Europe, USA, Canada, Australia, Japan

Cover: Foto ©Andreas Hilbeck / pixelio.de

More available books at **www.hansebooks.com**

HYMNS

OF

TER STEEGEN

AND OTHERS

TRANSLATED BY

FRANCES BEVAN

AUTHOR OF "THREE FRIENDS OF GOD," "MATELDA AND THE
CLOISTER OF HELLFDE," ETC. ETC.

SECOND SERIES

𝔏𝔬𝔫𝔡𝔬𝔫

JAMES NISBET & CO., LIMITED

22 BERNERS STREET, W.

PREFACE

FROM the writings of the "Friends of God"
of old time, most of the hymns that follow
have been taken. Those of Mechthild of
Hellfde, known also as Mechthild of Magde-
burg, may be found in her book, "Das
fliessende Licht der Gottheit," translated
from Low German into High German in the
year 1344, and discovered in High German
in the convent library of Einsiedeln in the
year 1861. Mechthild, supposed with much
reason to be the Matilda of Dante, belongs
to the evangelical witnesses of the middle
ages, known to us through Tauler, Suso,
and others of those called the "Friends of
God." How distinct was their witness to
the truth of the Gospel may be easily seen
by comparing their writings with those of
the true servants of God who remained under

the influence of Roman Catholicism only. A comparison of Thomas à Kempis with Tauler will serve as an instance of this contrast. In the case of the latter, the *present* possession and enjoyment of eternal life, and of the riches of Christ; in the case of the former, an earnest and true desire to *attain* to that possession. In the latter, forgiveness, peace, and joy, the starting-point; in the former, the goal, to be reached by strenuous effort. The joy of Heaven, Christ in glory, known and rejoiced in whilst here below, may be said to mark the Friends of God of old. And in our days is there not the same celestial mark set upon those who, having learnt the blessed truth that we have died with Christ, now rejoice in the fulness of life, in Him, and in His own, and find themselves already in the possession of the deepest joy of Heaven, having known the love of Christ which passeth knowledge? It is this link which connects true saints of old with those of our days, for of all alike it is said, "We have come unto Mount Zion, to the City

of God," even whilst walking on the earth,
despised and persecuted. Whilst we look
onward and forward to the day of the return
of Christ, to the final deliverance from all
that now hinders and clouds our enjoyment
of Him, have we not already that which
makes the desert to be to us as the garden
of the Lord? It was for this, God the Spirit
came down to us in His grace and love, and
whilst He takes of the things of Christ and
shows them to us, we know what are the
things which God has prepared for those
who love Him, and in the earnest of them
we rejoice. May the many voices who join
in praise for this everlasting and present
joy bring comfort and cheer to the hearts
of the pilgrims who are passing on to the
full realisation of all that is given us in
Christ!"

CONTENTS

FOR THE CHILDREN

HYMNS

IN HIS TABERNACLE

"One thing have I desired of the Lord, that will I seek
after; that I may dwell in the house of the Lord all
the days of my life, to behold the beauty of the Lord."
—Ps. xxvii. 4.

Not built with hands is that fair radiant
    chamber
Of God's untroubled rest—
Where Christ awaits to lay His weary-
    hearted
In stillness on His breast.
Not built on sands of time or place to perish,
    When tempests roar—
But on the mighty Rock of Ages founded,
    It stands for evermore—
Not only in a day of distant dawning,
    When past are desert years,
But now, amidst the turmoil and the battle,
    The mocking and the tears,

A

That Chamber still and stately waits us ever,
    That sacred pure retreat—
That rest in Arms of tenderest enfoldings,
    That welcome passing sweet.
O Home of God my Father's joy and glad-
        ness,
    O riven Veil whereby I enter in !
There can my soul forget the grave, the
        weeping,
    The weariness and sin.
O Chamber, all thine agate windows opened
    To face the radiant east—
O holy Temple, where the saints are singing,
    Where Jesus is the Priest—
Illumined with the everlasting glory,
    Still with the peace of God's eternal Now,
Thou, God, my Rest, my Refuge, and my
        Tower—
    My Home art Thou.

                                        T. S. M.

ARRIVED

"Ye are come unto Mount Zion, and unto the city of the living God, the heavenly Jerusalem."—HEB. xii. 22.

WE are come unto Mount Zion,
On Thy holy hill we stand,
The crusaders whose march is ended,
The risen and the ascended,
All hail! Immanuel's land!

We are come unto the City,
Where our living God art Thou ;
Thou Who barest our sin and sorrow,
Who comest in joy to-morrow,
Thou communest with us now—

To Jerusalem the golden,
To the Gates of Praise we come,
To the walls of Thy strong salvation,
The chambers of consolation,
The wandering ones brought home—

To the companies of Angels
   We declare Thy glorious grace—
In the stoles by Thy Blood made whiter,
And crowned with a radiance brighter
   Than they who behold Thy Face.

We are come to the great Assembly
   Of the first-born sons of God,
The enrolled in the ancient ages,
In love's everlasting pages,
   Names registered there in Blood.

With our God, the Judge of all men,
   Undismayed, unshamed we meet,
For the tears of a sinner shriven,
The kisses of lips forgiven,
   For ever anoint His Feet.

With the spirits pure and holy
   Of the saints of ancient years,
Of the loved ones whom death made dearer,
The absent who yet are nearer,
   We worship amidst our tears.

We are come unto Thee, Lord Jesus,
  We have found Thee where Thou art ;
In Thy still pavilion hiding,
For ever in peace abiding—
  Our eternal Home Thy heart.

We are come where the Priest has sprinkled
  On the everlasting throne,
On the Ark where Thy glory dwelleth,
The Blood that for ever telleth
  The work is done.

T. S. M.

THE HEARING EAR

"The sheep hear His Voice."—JOHN x. 3.

O HOLY and mighty and marvellous Word
  That speakest ever to me ;
As of old in the silence of Eden heard
  In the shade of the sacred Tree—
O Word from the depths of the ancient years,
  From deserts Thy pilgrims trod,
From the hidden chambers of saints and
    seers,
  From the secret place of God—

From the well of Sychar, the gate of Nain,
 From the winds of the midnight sea,
Thou speakest in marvellous songs again
 In the stillness of night to me.
From the noonday darkness the solemn Voice
 Tells of my judgment borne—
And it calls to my soul to sing and rejoice
 From the glow of the First-day morn.
Unsilenced yet to the ear that hears,
 Thou Voice of eternal bliss,
Thou speakest in speech that is deeper than tears,
 And sweet as the Father's kiss.
In Heaven the marvellous song ascends,
 And in chambers mean and dim,
Where over the dead the mourner bends,
 There steals the eternal Hymn.

T. S. M.

THE SECOND TOUCH

"After that He put His hands again upon his eyes, and
made him look up."—MARK viii. 25.

Lo! a Hand amidst the darkness
  Clasped mine own—
Led me forth the blind and helpless,
  Led me forth alone;
From the crowd and from the clamour
  To a silent place;
Touched mine eyes—I looked upon Him—
  Saw Him face to face.
Saw Him, as the dawning swiftly risen
  O'er the valleys grey;
I had passed from midnight of my prison
  Forth into the day.
Lo! again His mighty Hand hath touched me,
  Touched the eyes so dim;
Radiant in the noontide of His Heaven
  Look they now on Him.
Where He is, I see Him and I know Him;
  Where He is I am,
In the Light that is the Love eternal,
  Light that is the Lamb.

"Go not back," so spake He, "to the
    city
Where men know Me not—
Tell not there the mystery and the wonder
    I have wrought.
Go unto thy Home, O My beloved
    To thy Home and Mine ;
Hear the blessed welcome of My Father,
    'All I have is thine.'"
Therefore am I journeying to the Father,
    And He walks with me
Over mountains, through the pastures of His
    valleys,
        O'er the sea—
And upwards through the heavens where
    His City
Burneth, gloweth with the light
Of the glory of the gems that He has
    gathered
    In the caverns of the night.
Already come the sounds of harps and
    singing
    When the winds arise,
And the joy of His espousals glows as
    morning
    Arisen in His eyes.

See ye nought of Him? His glory and His
  beauty?
O eyes so sad and dim?
Still—hearken—He is passing—He is passing—
    Come unto Him.

C. P. C.

THE POWER

"Not by might, nor by power, but by My Spirit, saith
the Lord of hosts."—ZECH. iv. 6.

REST from longing and desire
  O thou weary heart!
Dost thou ween thy choice has been
Not the lower but the higher,
  Thine the better part?
And therefore dost thou long with bitter
    longing
  From the day dawn to the night,
For the holiness, the rest of His beloved
  Who walk with Him in white?
Thou art wearied with the striving and the
    yearning

For the crown that thou wouldst win ;
Thou hast learnt but thine immensity of
  weakness,
But the mystery of thy sin.
Beloved, the Lord spake to me in comfort
  When thus it was with me—
" Wert thou cast all alone upon thy mantle,
  All alone upon the sea—
Nought round thee but immensity of waters,
  No strength in thee to swim,
How, seeing only God in Heaven above
  thee,
Wouldst thou cast thyself on Him ? "
Therefore thank Him for thy helplessness,
  beloved,
  And if thou needs must long,
Let it be but for the rest of utter weakness,
  In the Arms for ever strong.
Long only that He make thee bare and
  empty—
  Take all that is thine own,
Thy prowess, and thy strength, and thine
  endeavour,
  And leave thee God alone.
In the stillness of that peace the work is
  ended

By Him, and not by thee;
The end of *His* desire and His longing
To see thee stand in stainless white before
    Him
Is that which needs must be.

J. TAULER, † 1361.

THE BLESSED COUNTRY

The wilderness and the solitary place shall be glad for
them; and the desert shall rejoice, and blossom as tho
rose."—Is. xxxv. 1.

O GLAD the wilderness for me,
    And glad the solitary place,
Since Thou hast made mine eyes to see,
    To see Thy Face.

Not heavenly fields, but desert sands
    Rejoice and blossom as the rose;
For through the dry and thirsty lands
    Thy River flows.

O Way beside that living tide,
    The Way, the Truth, the Life art Thou;
I drink, and I am satisfied,
    Now, even now.

Eternal joy already won,
Eternal songs already given;
For long ago the work was done
That opened Heaven.

C. P. C.

THE DWELLING OF THE LORD

"They said unto Him, Master, where dwellest Thou? He
saith unto them, Come and see."—JOHN i. 38, 39.

Now — borne upon the still, the boundless
deep,
By tempest never stirred,
The peaceful sea where song and minstrelsy
From shores that in the golden morning
sleep
Alone are heard.

Now—hidden in His secret place, afar
Within the sheltering Home—
Apart as in the glory of a star
Where all the strifes that madden and that
mar
May never come.

Now—o'er the dark and solitary ways
  Borne onward on His breast,
Through windings of the strange and tangled
    maze,
Through weary nights, and through the
    changing days,
      At rest—at rest.

Now—lips unskilful fain would tell the bliss
  The heart in secret shares—
The meeting, and the welcome, and the kiss,
The blessed marvels and the mysteries
      His love prepares.

Now—holy cloisters closed to strife and sin
  Where Angels walk in white—
And blessed saints adoring enter in,
Their everlasting anthems to begin
      In songs of night.

Now—O Beloved Lord, Thy risen ones,
  In peace we walk with Thee;
Beyond the graves we dwell, beyond the
    suns;
Beside the fountain whence the River runs
      At last to be!

C. P. C.

RISEN AND ASCENDED

"While He blessed them, He was parted from them, and carried up into Heaven."—LUKE xxiv. 51.

ALL hail! O glorious Son of God,
In triumph risen again—
All heaven resounds with joyful laud
The songs of ransomed men ;
The mighty chains of death are riven,
The Risen Christ is throned in Heaven.

Before thee all the shining hosts
The mighty Angels bend ;
Thy saved ones from a thousand coasts
Their psalms of victory blend—
I join that song so passing sweet,
I cast my crown before Thy Feet.

O joy ! the second Adam stands
Within God's Paradise—
No longer barred by flaming brands
The shining pathway lies—
Within, the glorious Head has passed ;
Each member must be there at last.

Behind us lie the cross and grave,
   Before, eternal bliss ;
There blossoms from the garden cave
   The Tree of Righteousness,
The Face that shame and spitting bore
Is crowned with radiance evermore.

With Mary, O my Lord, I bow
   In rapture at Thy Feet;
In spirit humbly kiss them now
   And soon in presence sweet ;
My name upon Thy lips divine
The lips that tell me " Thou art mine."

Thou livest far from earthly strife
   In God's eternal peace—
And there with Thee is hid my life,
   And there my wanderings cease ;
The secret place where still and blest
I rest in Thine eternal rest.

                              G. Ter Steegen.

MARAH

"The Lord showed him a tree, which when he had
cast into the waters, the waters were made
sweet."—EXOD. xv. 25.

MANY sorrows hard and bitter,
  Many comforts sweet and soft ;
Thus my cry as joyful singing
  Evermore shall mount aloft.
Song of marvellous rejoicing
  As in Heaven the blessed sing,
For the love of Christ has filled me
  With His sweetest plenishing.
Joy no thought of man conceiveth,
  Howsoever deep his lore ;
None can tell but he who hath it,
  Hath it now and evermore.
Ill they spake, " Can God provide us,
  Cheer amidst the wilderness ? "
He a feast of joy has furnished,
  Feast of sweetness, love, and bliss.
In the desert Bread He giveth,
  So that nought we crave beside,
Raineth the delight of Heaven,
  We are more than satisfied.

Thus my sorrow turns to music
And my cry to sweetest song ;
Weeping to eternal gladness,
Night is short—the Day is long.

RICHARD ROLLE, † 1349.

THE HOME OF THE SOUL

"Giving thanks unto the Father, which hath made
us meet to be partakers of the inheritance of the
saints in light."—COL. i. 12.

THE mind saith to the soul—
" In the glory of God no foot hath trod ;
A devouring Fire dread to see ;
In the blinding light of the face of God
        No soul can be.
For thou knowest that all high Heaven is
        bright
With a glory beyond the sun,
With the radiance of the saints in light,
And the fount of that Light is one.
From the breath of the everlasting God,
From the mouth of the Man Divine,
From the counsel of God the Holy Ghost
Doth that awful glory shine.

B

Soul, couldst thou abide for an hour alone
  In the burning fire around His throne?

And the soul makes answer—

The fish drowns not in the mighty sea,
  The bird sinks not in the air,
The gold in the furnace fire may be,
  And is yet more radiant there.
For God to each of His creatures gave
  The place to its nature known;
And shall it not be that my heart should crave
  For that which is mine own?
For my nature seeketh her dwelling-place,
  That only, and none other;
The child must joy in the Father's face,
  The brethren in the Brother.
To the bridal chamber goeth the bride,
  For love is her home and rest;
And shall not I in His light abide,
  When I lean upon His breast?

.   .   .   .

And she who is beloved with love untold,
  Thus goes to Him Who is divinely fair,
In His still Chamber of unsullied gold,
  And love all pure, all holy, greets her
    there—

The love of His eternal Godhead high,
The love of His divine Humanity.
Then speaketh He and saith, " Beloved one,
What wouldst thou ?   It is thine.
From self shalt thou go forth for evermore,
For thou art Mine.
O soul ! no angel for an hour might dream
Of all the riches that I give to thee;
The glory and the beauty that beseem
The heritage of life that is in Me.
Yet satisfied, thou shalt for ever long,
So sweeter shall be thine eternal song."
O Lord my God, so small, so poor am I,
And great, Almighty, O my God, art
Thou !
" Yet art thou joined to Christ eternally,
My love a changeless everlasting NOW."
And thus the joyful soul is still
At rest in God's eternal will ;
And she is His, and thus delighteth He
Her own to be.

MECHTHILD OF HELLFDE, † 1277.

THE FOOTSTEPS

"Ye shall indeed drink of the cup that I drink of."
—MARK x. 39.

BEHOLD, My bride, how fair My mouth, Mine
    eyes ;
My heart is glowing fire, My hand is
    grace—
And see how swift My foot, and follow Me.
For thou with Me shalt scorned and mar-
    tyred be,
Betrayed by envy, tempted in the wilds,
And seized by hate, and bound by cal-
    umny ;
And they shall bind thine eyes lest thou
    shouldst see,
By hiding Mine eternal truth from thee.
And they shall scourge thee with the world's
    despite,
And shrive thee with the ban of doom and
    dread,
For penance thy dishonoured head shall
    smite,
By mockery thou to Herod shalt be led,

By misery left forlorn—
And bound by want, and by temptation
  crowned,
  And spit upon by scorn.
The loathing of thy sin thy cross shall be,
Thy crucifixion, crossing of thy will ;
The nails, obedience that shall fasten thee,
And love shall wound, and steadfastness
  shall slay,
    Yet thou shalt love Me still.
The spear shall pierce thy heart ; *My* life
  shall be
The life that lives and moves henceforth in
  thee.
Then as a conqueror loosened from the
  cross,
Laid in the grave of nothingness and
  loss,
Thou shalt awaken, and be borne above
Upon the breath of Mine Almighty love.

MECHTHILD OF HELLFDE, † 1277.

IN THE GARDEN OF GOD

"Tell me, O Thou whom my soul loveth, where Thou
    feedest, where Thou makest Thy flock to rest at
    noon."—CANT. i. 7.

WHEN mine eyes are dim with weeping,
    And my tongue with grief is dumb ;
And it is as if Thou wert sleeping,
    When my heart calleth, " Come ; "
When I hunger with bitter hunger
        O Lord for Thee,
Where art Thou then, Belovèd ?
        Speak, speak to me—
" I am where I was in the ancient days,
    I in Myself must be ;
In all things I am, and in every place,
    For there is no change in Me.
Where the sun is My Godhead, throned
        above,
    For thee, O Mine own I wait;
I wait for thee in the Garden of love,
    Till thou comest irradiate,

With the light that shines from My Face
    divine,
And I pluck the flowers for thee;
They are thine, beloved, for they are Mine,
    And thou art one with Me.
In the tender grass by the waters still
    I have made thy resting-place ;
Thy rest shall be sweet in My holy will,
    And sure in My changeless grace—
And I bend for thee the holy Tree,
    Where blossoms the mystic Rod,
The highest of all the trees that be
    In the Paradise of God.
And thou of that Tree of life shalt eat,
    Of the Life that is in Me ;
Thou shalt feed on the fruit that is good for
    meat,
    And passing fair to see.
There, overshadowed by mighty wings
    Of the Holy Spirit's peace,
Beyond the sorrow of earthly things,
    The toil and the tears shall cease.
And there beneath the eternal Tree
    I will teach thy lips to sing,
The sweet new song that is strange to thee
    In the land of thy banishing.

They follow the Lamb where'er He goes
  To whom it is revealed ;
The pure and the undefiled are those,
  The ransomed and the sealed.
Thou shalt learn the speech and the music
    rare,
  And thou shalt sing as they,
Not only there in my garden fair,
  But here belovèd, to-day."
O Lord, a faint and a feeble voice
  Is mine in this house of clay,
But Thy love hath made my lips rejoice,
  And I can sing and say,
" I am pure, O Lord, for Thou art pure,
  Thy love and mine are one ;
And my robe is white, for Thine is white,
  And brighter than the sun.
Thy mouth and mine can know no moan,
  No note of man's sad mirth,
But the everlasting joy alone
  Unknown to songs of earth ;
And for ever fed on that living Tree,
  I will sing the song of Thy love with Thee."

MECHTHILD OF HELLFDE, † 1277.

DWELLING IN LOVE

"We love Him, because He first loved us."
—1 JOHN iv. 19.

I REJOICE that I cannot but love Him,
  Because He first loved me ;
I would that measureless, changeless,
      My love might be ;
A love unto death and for ever ;
  For, soul, He died for thee.
Give thanks that for thee He delighted
  To leave His glory on high ;
For thee to be humbled, forsaken,
      For thee to die.
Wilt thou render Him love for His
    loving ?
Wilt thou die for Him who died ?
And so by thy dying and living
  Shall Christ be magnified.
And deep in the fiery stream that flows
    From God's high throne,
In the burning tide that for ever glows
  Of the marvellous love unknown ;

For ever, O soul, thou shalt burn and glow,
  And thou shalt sing and say,
" I need no call at His feet to fall,
  For I cannot turn away.
I am the captive led along
With the joy of His triumphal song;
In the depths of love do I love and move,
  I joy to live or to die;
For I am borne on the tide of His love
      To all eternity: "
The foolishness of the fool is this,
The sorrow sweeter than joy to miss.

MECHTHILD OF HELLFDE, † 1277.

THE GIFT

"There came no more such abundance of spices as
    those which the queen of Sheba gave to King
    Solomon."—1 KINGS x. 10.

" WHAT dost thou bring me, O my Queen?
  Love maketh thy steps to fly."
Lord, to Thee my jewel I bring,
  Greater than mountains high;

Broader than all the earth's broad lands,
Heavier than the ocean sands,
   And higher it is than the sky :
Deeper it is than the depths of the sea,
   And fairer than the sun,
Unreckoned, as if the stars could be
   All gathered into one.
"O thou My Godhead's image fair,
   Thou Eve from Adam framed,
My flesh, My bone, My life to share,
My Spirit's diadem to wear,
   How is thy jewel named ? "

Lord, it is called my heart's desire,
   From the world's enchantments won ;
I have borne it afar through flood and fire
   And will yield it up to none ;
But the burden I can bear no more—
Where shall I lay it up in store ?

"There is no treasure-house but this,
   My heart divine, My Manhood's breast ;
There shall My Spirit's sacred kiss
   Fill thee with rest."
MECHTHILD OF HELLFDE, † 1277.

A SONG IN THE NIGHT

"Then took Mary a pound of ointment of spikenard,
very costly, and anointed the feet of Jesus."—
JOHN xii. 3.

O JESUS Lord, most fair, most passing sweet,
    In darkest hours revealed in love to me,
In those dark hours I fall before Thy feet,
        I sing to Thee.
I join the song of love, and I adore
    With those who worship Thee for ever-
    more.
Thou art the Sun of every eye,
    The Gladness everywhere,
The guiding Voice for ever nigh,
    The Strength to do and bear;
The sacred Lore of wisdom's store,
    The Life of life to all,
The Order mystic, marvellous
    In all things great and small.
Thy love hast Thou told from the days of old,
    Thou hast written my name in Thy Book
    divine;

Engraved on Thy hands and Thy feet it
    stands,
    And on Thy side as a sign ;
O glorious Man in the garden of God,
    Thy sacred Manhood is mine.
I kneel on the golden floor of Heaven
    With my box of ointment sweet,
Grant unto me, Thy much forgiven,
    To kiss and anoint Thy feet.
" Where wilt thou find that ointment rare,
    O My belovèd one ? "
Thou brakest my heart, and didst find it
    there,
    Rest sweetly there alone.
" There is no embalming so sweet to Me
    As to dwell, my well-belovèd, in thee."
Lord, take me home to Thy palace fair,
    So will I ever anoint Thee there.
" I will, but My plighted troth saith, ' Wait,'
    And My love saith, ' Work to-day ;'
My meekness saith, ' Be of low estate,'
    And My longing, ' Watch and pray ;'
My shame and sorrow say, ' Bear My cross ;'
    My song saith, ' Win the crown ;'
My guerdon saith, ' All else is loss ;'
    My patience saith, ' Be still ;'

Till thou shalt lay the burden down,
    Then, when I will.
Then, beloved, the crown and palm,
    And then the music and the psalm ;
And the cup of joy My hand shall fill
    Till it overflow ;
And with singing I strike the harp of gold
    I have tuned below.
The harp I tune in desolate years
    Of sorrow and tears,
Till a music sweet the chords repeat,
    Which all the heavens shall fill;
For the holy courts of God made meet,
    Then, when I will."

           MECHTHILD OF HELLFDE, † 1277.

THINGS SEEN AND HEARD

" My Beloved is mine, and I am His; He feedeth among
the lilies."—CANT. ii. 16.

THOU hast shone within this soul of mine,
    As the sun on a shrine of gold ;
When I rest my heart, O Lord, on Thine,
    My bliss is manifold.

My soul is the gem on Thy diadem,
　And my marriage robe Thou art ;
If aught could sever my heart from Thine,
　The sorrow beyond all sorrows were mine,
　　Alone and apart.
Could I not find Thy love below,
Then would my soul as a pilgrim go
　To Thy holy land above ;
There would I love Thee as I were fain
　With everlasting love.
Now have I sung my tuneless song,
　But I hearken, Lord, for Thine ;
So shall a music, sweet and strong,
　　Pass into mine.
" I am the Light, and the lamp thou art ;
　The River, and thou the thirsty land ;
To thee thy sighs have drawn My heart,
　And ever beneath thee is My Hand.
And when thou weepest it needs must be
Within Mine arms that encompass thee ;
Thy heart from Mine can none divide,
For one are the Bridegroom and the Bride ;
It is sweet, beloved, for Me and thee
To wait for the Day that is to be."
O Lord, with hunger and thirst I wait,
With longing before Thy golden gate,

Till the Day shall dawn
When from Thy lips divine have passed
   The sacred words that none may hear
But the soul that, loosed from the earth at
     last,
      Hath laid her ear
To the mouth that speaks in the still sweet
     morn
     Apart and alone——
Then shall the secret of love be told
   The mystery known.

MECHTHILD OF HELLFDE, † 1277.

MADE ONE

" He that is joined unto the Lord is one spirit."
—1 COR. vi. 17.

THE mouth of the Lord hath spoken,
   Hath spoken a mighty word ;
My sinful heart it hath broken,
   Yet sweeter I never heard ;
" Thou, thou art, O soul, My deep desire
   And My love's eternal bliss :
Thou art the rest where leaneth My breast,
   And My mouth's most holy kiss.

Thou art the treasure I sought and found,
　　Rejoicing over thee ;
I dwell in thee, and with thee am I crowned,
　　And thou dost dwell in Me.
Thou art joined to Me, O Mine own, for
　　ever,
　　And nearer thou canst not be—
Shall aught on earth or in Heaven sever
　　Myself from Me ? ”
　　　　　MECHTHILD OF HELLFDE, † 1277.

BENEATH HIS BANNER

“ Thine are we, David, and on thy side, thou son of
Jesse.”—1 CHRON. xii. 18.

'TWIXT God and thee but love shall be ;
'Twixt earth and thee distrust and fear,
'Twixt sin and thee shall be hate and
　　war ;
And hope shall be 'twixt Heaven and thee
　　Till night is o'er.
　　　　　MECHTHILD OF HELLFDE, † 1277.

THE HIGHWAY

"The Lord God is my strength, and He will make my
feet like hinds' feet, and He will make me to walk
upon mine high places."—HAB. iii. 19.

IT is a wondrous and a lofty road
  Wherein the faithful soul must tread,
And by the seeing there the blind are led,
  The senses by the soul acquaint with God.
On that high path the soul is free,
  She knows no care nor ill,
For all God wills desireth she,
      And blessed is His will.

MECHTHILD OF HELLFDE, † 1277.

THE BRIDE, THE LAMB'S WIFE

'Whom have I in Heaven but Thee? and there is none upon
earth that I desire beside Thee."—Ps. lxxiii. 25.

THUS speaks the Bride whose feet have trod
  The chamber of eternal rest,
The secret treasure-house of God,
  Where God is manifest :

"Created things, arise and flee,
Ye are but sorrow and care to me."
This wide, wide world, so rich and fair,
Thou sure canst find thy solace there?
"Nay, 'neath the flowers the serpent glides,
Amidst the bravery envy hides."
And is not Heaven enough for thee?
"Were God not there, 'twere a tomb to
    Me."
O Bride, the saints in glory shine;
Can *they* not fill this heart of thine?
"Nay, were the Lamb their Light with-
    drawn,
The saints in gloom would weep and
    mourn."
Can the Son of God not comfort thee?
"Yea, Christ and none besides for me.
For mine is a soul of noble birth,
That needeth more than Heaven and earth;
And the breath of God must draw me in
To the Heart that was riven for my sin.
For the Sun of the Godhead pours His rays
Through the crystal depths of His Man-
    hood's grace,
And the Spirit sent by Father and Son
Hath filled my soul, and my heart hath won :

And the longing and love are past and gone,
For all that is less than God alone—
God only, sweet to this heart of mine,
O wondrous death that is life divine!"

Mechthild of Hellfde, † 1277.

ECCE HOMO

"Look unto Me, and be ye saved, all the ends of the
earth."—Is. xlv. 22.

Wilt thou, sinner, be converted?
   Christ the Lord of glory see
By His own denied, deserted,
   Bleeding, bound, and scourged for thee.
Look again, O soul, behold Him
   On the cross uplifted high ;
See the precious life-blood flowing,
   See the tears that dim His eye.
Love has pierced the heart that brake,
   Loveless sinner, for thy sake.
Hearken till thy heart is broken
   To His cry so sad and sweet,
Hearken to the hammer smiting
   Nails that pierce His hands and feet.

See the side whence flows the fountain
  Of His love and life divine,
Riven by a hand unthankful—
  Lo! that hand is thine.
See the crown of thorns adorning
  God's belovèd, holy Son;
Then fall down in bitter mourning,
  Weep for that which *thou* hast done.
Thank Him that His heart was willing
  So to die for love of thee;
Thank Him for the joy that maketh
  This world's joy but gall to be.
And till thou in Heaven adore Him
  Fight for Him in knightly guise,
Joy in shame and scorn and sorrow;
  Glorious is the prize!
            MECHTHILD OF HELLFDE, † 1277.

THE EXCHANGE

"I count all things but loss for the excellency of the
  knowledge of Christ Jesus my Lord."—PHIL. iii. 8.

IF the world were mine and all its store,
  And were it of crystal gold;
Could I reign on its throne for evermore
  From the ancient days of old,

An empress noble and fair as day,
  O gladly might it be,
That I might cast it all away ;
  Christ, only Christ for me.
For Christ my Lord my spirit longs,
  For Christ, my Saviour dear ;
The joy and sweetness of my songs
  The whilst I wander here—
O Lord, my spirit fain would flee
From the lonely desert away to Thee.

MECHTHILD OF HELLFDE, † 1277.

SEVEN-FOLD JOY

"Seven times a day do I praise Thee because of Thy
righteous judgments."—Ps. cxix. 164.

I BRING unto Thy grace a seven-fold praise,
  Thy wondrous love I bless—
I praise, remembering my sinful days,
    My worthlessness.
I praise that I am waiting, Lord, for Thee,
  When, all my wanderings past,
Thyself wilt bear me, and wilt welcome me
    To home at last.

I praise Thee that for Thee I long and pine,
    For Thee I ever yearn ;
I praise Thee that such fitful love as mine
    Thou dost not spurn ;
I praise Thee for the hour when first I saw
    The glory of Thy face,
Here dimly, but in fulness evermore
    In that high place.
I praise Thee for a mystery unnamed,
    Unuttered here below ;
Unspeakable in words the lips have framed,
    Yet passing sweet to know.
It is the still, the everlasting tide,
    The stream of Love Divine,
That from the heart of God for evermore
      Flows into mine.
To that deep joy that bindeth Heart to
    heart
    In one eternal love,
A still small stream that flows unseen below
    An endless sea above,
To that high love, that fathomless delight,
    No thought of man may reach ;
And yet beyond it is a seven-fold bliss
    Most holy of God's holy mysteries,
      Untold in speech.

Faith only hath beheld that secret place,
  Faith only knows how great, how high
    how fair,
The Temple where the Lord unveils His
    Face
  To His belovèd there.
O how unfading is that pure delight!
How full the joy of that exhaustless tide
Which flows for ever in its glorious might,
    So still, so wide!
And deep we drink with sweet eternal
    thirst,
  With lips for ever eager as at first,
    Yet ever satisfied.

MECHTHILD OF HELLFDE, † 1277.

CALLED UP

"Precious in the sight of the Lord is the death of His
saints."—Ps. cxvi. 15.

HE laid him down upon the breast of God
  In measureless delight—
Enfolded in the tenderness untold,
  The sweetness infinite.

MECHTHILD OF HELLFDE, † 1277.

CHANGE OF RAIMENT

" Behold, I have caused thine iniquity to pass from
thee, and I will clothe thee with change of raiment.
And I said, Let them set a fair mitre upon his
head. So they set a fair mitre upon his head, and
clothed him with garments."—ZECH. iii. 4, 5.

LORD JESUS, all my sin and guilt
  Love laid of old on Thee,
Thy love the cross and sorrow willed,
  Love undeserved by me.
The victory over death and hell
  Thou, Lord, for me didst win ;
And Thou hast nailed upon Thy Cross
  All, all my sin.

The way into the Holiest Place
  Stands open now to me ;
Where I can see Thy glorious Face,
  Nor tremble thus to see.
For as I am to Thee I come,
  I clasp Thy blessed Feet,
And learn the mystery of love
  So deep, so sweet.

Enfolded, O my Lord, in Thee,
And hid in Thee I rest,
Enwrapped in Christ's own purity
Secure upon Thy breast.
Had I an Angel's raiment—fair
With heavenly gems unpriced,
That glorious garb I would not wear,
My robe is Christ.

G. TER STEEGEN.

ABOVE AND BELOW

"As sorrowful, yet alway rejoicing."—2 COR. vi. 10.

IN the bosom of the Father,
Centre of His endless love,
In the light and in the glory,
Thus in Christ I dwell above.

Filling up His bitter sufferings,
Drinking of His cup of woe,
And rejoicing as I do it,
Thus with Christ I walk below.

There above I rest, untroubled,
  All my service to adore ;
Cross and shame and death and sorrow
  Left behind for evermore.

Therefore am I never weary
  Journeying onward through the waste ;
And the bitter Marah waters
  Have but sweetness to my taste.

While He tells the wondrous secret
  Of His perfect love to me,
While His heart's exhaustless fulness
  In His blessed face I see ;

Can there be but joy and glory
  In His Cross and shame below ?
Sweet each mark of His rejection ;
  Where His steps are, I must go.

One the path, and one the sorrow—
  Path the angels cannot tread ;
Sorrow giving sweet assurance
  We are members, He the Head,

Blessed path that ends to-morrow
　In the place where He is gone ;
Thus, the silver trumpets sounding,
　Through the waste we journey on.

P. G.

BROUGHT NIGH

"Riches of His grace."—EPH. i. 7.
"Riches of His glory."—EPH. iii. 16.

RICH, our God, art Thou in mercy,
　Dead in sins were we,
When Thy great love rested on us,
　Sinners, dear to Thee.

Blessed path of grace that led us
　From the depths of death
To the fair eternal mansions
　Quickened by Thy breath.

Riches of Thy grace have brought us
　There, in Christ, to Thee ;
Riches of Thy glory make us
　Thy delight to be.

Not alone the stream that cleansed us
　Flowed from Jesus dead,
Tides of glory now are flowing
　From our living Head.

Down to us from Christ in Heaven
　Those bright rivers run—
In His lowest saint and feeblest,
　God beholds His Son.

He with deep delight is tracing
　Every feature fair
Of His Son, His well-belovèd,
　Throned beside Him there.

And those lines of glorious beauty
　Here His eye can see,
Back to God in light reflected,
　Christ revealed in me.

Gazing on the cloudless glory
　Of the Lord we love,
Where unveiled He fills with radiance
　Those bright courts above,

Day by day a change is passing
    O'er each lifted brow,
Soon to shine like Christ in glory,
    Though so dimly now.

Evermore that light transforms us
    In the Father's sight,
Not His love alone our portion,
    But His full delight.

Not because of guilt, but glory,
    Doth His love provide
That fair robe so well beseeming
    Christ's unspotted Bride.

Fair amidst His new creation
    Formed from Christ alone,
God in us His Son beholding,
    Rests, the work is done.

Wondrous riches of the glory
    Won in shame and blood,
And from heaven outpoured in fulness,
    Endless love of God.

W. R.

THE SONG OF HIS JOY

"He will save, He will rejoice over thee with joy; He
will rest in His love, He will joy over thee with
singing."—ZEPH. iii. 17.

WONDROUS joy, Thy joy, Lord Jesus,
   Deep, eternal, pure, and bright—
Thou alone the Man of Sorrows,
   Thus couldst tell of joy aright.

Lord, we know that joy, that gladness,
   Which in fulness Thou hast given—
Sharing all that countless treasure,
   We on earth with Thee in Heaven.

. . . Even as He went before us
   Through the wilderness below.
So, in strength unworn, unfailing,
   Onward also would we go.

All the earth a desert round Him,
   All His springs in God alone ;
Every heart, save God's heart only,
   Making discord with His own.

There to walk alone, rejoicing—
    Through the ruin and the sin ;
Darkness of the midnight round Him,
    Glory of God's love within.

From no lower fountain flowing
    Than the heart of God above,
All the gladness of that glory,
    All the power of that love.

Onward to the cross rejoicing,
    Where all powers of evil met,
Giving thanks 'midst deepest darkness
    That God's love was deeper yet.

Then ascended in the glory,
    By that love's unfailing spring,
There to sing the song of triumph,
    There the song of songs to sing.

Hearken to that hymn of glory
    Filling all the holy place,
Golden psalm of Him who looketh
    On the Father's blessed face.

Voice of measureless rejoicing,
  Joy unmingled, deep and clear,
Wonder to the listening Heavens,
  Music to the Father's ear.

Won in travail of His Spirit,
  Agony, and shame, and blood,
That blest place beside the Father,
  Nearest to the heart of God.

Won for *me!* my praises leading,
  Jesus sings that song divine;
All His joy my own for ever,
  All His peace for ever mine.

What though drought be all around me,
  Desert land on every side—
With that spring of love and gladness
  Shall I not be satisfied?

T. P.

D

THE HIDDEN PATH

"There is a path which no fowl knoweth, and which
the vulture's eye hath not seen."—JOB xxviii. 7.

ONE place have I in heaven above
The glory of His throne—
On this dark earth, whence He is gone,
I have one place alone,
And if His rest in Heaven I know,
I joy to find His path below,

We meet to own that place alone
Around the broken bread—
The dead whose life is hid with Christ
Remembering Jesus dead.
For us has set the earthly light,
Above, the glory ; here, the night.

And dear as is His place on high,
His footsteps are below,
Where He has gone through scorn and
wrong,
There also would I go.
Lord, where Thou diedst I would die,
For where Thou livest, there am I.

One lonely path across the waste,
  Thy lowly path of shame ;
I would adore Thy wondrous grace
  That I should tread the same.
The Stranger and the Alien, Thou—
And I the stranger, alien, now.

Thy Cross a mighty barrier stands
  Between the world and me—
Not yielding with reluctant hands,
  But glorying to be free,
From that which now is dung and dross,
  Beside Thy Glory, and Thy Cross.

I see Thee there amidst the light,
  The Father's blessed Son ;
I know that I in Thee am there,
  That light and love mine own.
What has this barren world to give,
  If there in Thy deep joy I live?

Sent hither from that glorious Home,
  As Thou wert sent before,
Of that great love from whence I come
  To witness evermore,
For this would I count all things loss,
  Thy joy, Thy glory, and Thy Cross.   T. P.

THE PEARL

"When he had found one pearl of great price, he
went and sold all that he had, and bought it."—
MATT. xiii. 46.

TALE of tenderness unfathomed
Told by God to me—
Tale of love, mysterious, awful—
Thus God's love must be.

God the Seeker—one fair image
Ever in His thought,
Pure, and radiant, and faultless,
Yet He found it not.

Not amongst His holy Angels,
Was there one so bright;
Not amongst His stars of glory
Dwelt His heart's delight.

Yet there was a depth unfathomed
In a lonely place ;
One great deep of endless sorrow
Darkness on its face.

Restless sea of black pollution
　Moaning evermore,
Weary waves for ever breaking
　On a barren shore.

There below in midnight darkness,
　Under those wild waves,
Lies the treasure God is seeking,
　Jewel that He craves.

Down beneath those sunless waters
　He from Heaven has passed,
He has found His heart's desire,
　Found His pearl at last.

All He had His heart has given
　For that gem unpriced—
Such art thou, O ransomed sinner,
　Yea, for such is Christ.

C. P. C.

TER STEEGEN'S GOLDEN TIMEPIECE

JOHN xiii. 5.

6 P.M.

WILT Thou be the sinner's servant,
  Humble, loving Lord,
Wash my ways, and all my converse,
  Thought, and deed, and word.
Make me bend, the least and lowest,
  At my brethren's feet ;
Love saith, " As the task is meanest,
  Is the service sweet."

MATT. xxvi. 28.

7 P.M.

Givest thou Thyself, Lord Jesus,
  Thus my life to be?
Thy most precious Blood and Body
  Offered up for me ?
Thou, O Lord, my food eternal
  My eternal feast—
All my hunger stilled for ever,
  All my thirst appeased.

JOHN xvii. 9, 20.

8 P.M.

Great High Priest whose prayers are music
    In the Father's ears,
I shall know their glorious answer
    Through eternal years.
Even now, O Lord, I know it,
    Made by love Divine,
One with Thee, henceforth, for ever,
    Therefore one with Thine.

JOHN xviii. 1.

9 P.M.

Lo! I see the shadow falling
    Awful in its gloom—
See Thee passing, O Belovèd,
    To Thy place of doom—
Mine the sin that veiled the glory,
    Thine the burden sore—
Yet, O world, so sweet that sorrow,
    Thou art sweet no more.

LUKE xxii. 41.

10 P.M.

Sorrowful, I see Thee kneeling
  That dread cup to take ;
Filled with wrath of my deserving
  Given Thee for my sake.
Yet to Thee how sweet the bitter,
  Sweet the Father's will !
Lord, may I, Thy love recalling,
  Suffer, and be still.

LUKE xxii. 44.

11 P.M

For Thine agony of weeping,
  For Thy sweat of Blood,
For Thy prayer that told the marvel
  Of the love of God ;
Lord, I thank Thee—still ascendeth
  That unceasing prayer,
Incense from my heart's still temple ;
  God's High Priest is there.

LUKE xxii 48.   ।

MIDNIGHT.

On ! the traitor's kiss to suffer
  On Thy lips Divine—
Yield Thyself to foemen, stricken
  By one word of Thine—
Give me, Lord, to bear rejoicing
  Cross and shame for Thee—
Meet with loving lips and gentle
  Him who hateth me.

JOHN xviii. 12.

1 A.M.

Unresisting, uncomplaining,
  Holy, harmless, calm ;
Driven, beaten, led to slaughter,
  God's unblemished Lamb—
Bind me in eternal fetters,
  Lead me, Thine alone ;
Silent when contempt and hatred
  Mark me for Thine own.

MARK xiv. 64.

2 A.M.

Lo! they judge Thee as a traitor,
　All the treachery mine—
Scourge Thee as a malefactor,
　Saviour Divine.
Search me, O my God, and try me,
　Cleanse my inmost will ;
Give to me, if men misjudge me,
　Patience sweet and still.

MARK xiv. 71.

3 A.M.

Peter hath denied Thee—wilder
　Rise the waters deep—
Smitten by Thine eyes of pity
　He hath fled to weep.
Make me strong, and true and faithful,
　All my strength in Thee ;
When my faithless steps would wander,
　Look Thou, Lord, on me.

Mark xv. 5.

4 A.M.

Silent midst the false accusers,
  Thou the Witness true ;
Proud, false lips revile and sentence
  Him they never knew.
I, the guilty one, acquitted
  By Thy lips Divine ;
Thine the curse and condemnation,
  Life and glory mine.

Mark xv. 19.

5 A.M.

Lo ! they mock Thee, spit upon Thee,
  Smite the Face of God ;
I shall stand in shining raiment,
  Whitened in Thy Blood—
Stand before Thy Throne of judgment
  Faultless, glad, and free ;
Grant me love to men who hate me
  As Thy love to me.

JOHN xix. 9.

6 A.M.

As a sheep before her shearers
 Dumb and still art Thou ;
For the kingdom and the glory
 Are not given Thee now.
Not for me the courts enchanted
 Of the world's delight—
With Thee in Thy palace gardens
 I shall walk in white.

JOHN xix. 16.

7 A.M.

Dragged from Thy belovèd city,
 Zion's holy hill,
Mirth of fools and song of drunkards,
 Thou art silent still.
Silently, O Lord, I follow
 In that path of shame,
Thy reproach and Thy dishonour
 Glory of my name.

JOHN xviii. 40.

8 A.M.

Thou, the Prince of Life, rejected,
  And the murderer claimed ;
Stripped and scourged by hands ungentle,
  Mocked by tongues untamed—
Strip from me, Lord, self's foul raiment,
  Clothe me with Thine own ;
I am fit for courts of Heaven,
  Clad in Christ alone.

JOHN xix. 2.

9 A.M.

With the crown of thorns they crown Thee,
  Scornfully they bow ;
On the Father's throne in glory
  Thou art seated now.
Mighty God, I bow before Thee,
  Thee, the Saviour King ;
Here, my joy to love and suffer ;
  There, to love and sing.

JOHN xix. 5.

10 A.M.

Mocked and spit upon, and bleeding,
　　Pilate leads Thee forth ;
In Thy face they see no beauty,
　　In Thy Blood no worth.
O despised and humble Jesus,
　　What, compared with Thee,
Are the glory and the beauty
　　Of all worlds to me.

JOHN xix. 16.

11 A.M.

Sentence passed on Thee, the guiltless
　　By a sinner's tongue—
I before Thy throne am speechless
　　I, who did the wrong.
By Thy holy lips acquitted,
　　Wondering, I go free—
Past for me are death and judgment,
　　Crucified with Thee.

JOHN xix. 17, 18

NOON.

Thou must bear Thy cross, Lord Jesus,
  With the robbers twain—
Wearied, bleeding, and forsaken
  In Thy shame and pain.
Taking up my cross I follow,
  All my glory this,
With Thee here to toil and suffer,
  Thy reproach my bliss.

LUKE xxiii. 33.

Lo ! unto the cross they nail Thee,
  Bitter gall prepare,
Those all-holy lips to moisten,
  Praying for them there.
When that wounded hand shall sweetly
  Pass that cup to me,
May it all the world embitter,
  Leave me naught but Thee.

LUKE xxiii. 43; JOHN xix. 25-27.

Hanging in Thy shame and anguish,
    Words of love and grace
Welcome the forgiven felon
    To Thy Holiest place—
Guide Thy mother, broken-hearted,
    To a home of rest—
Comfort him, who yester even
    Lay upon Thy Breast.

MATT. xxvii. 46; JOHN xix. 30.

In Thy direst need forsaken,
    Now the work is done—
Thou dost bow Thy Head to welcome
    Me, Thy wandering one—
Bend to kiss Thine own, Thy ransomed—
    In that kiss to die—
My Belovèd, Thine for ever,
    Thine alone am I.

JOHN xix. 34.

4 P.M.

From Thy side the blood and water
  Flow to cleanse my sin—
Rent the mystic veil of Heaven ;
  I have entered in.
Heart of love, to sinners open,
  Place where God can meet
His beloved, His priest anointed
  At His mercy seat.

JOHN xix. 41.

5 P.M.

New the grave wherein Thou liest
  Wound in linen fine—
I an old cold grave have found Thee,
  This poor heart of mine.
So shall that dark grave be glorious,
  New, and pure, and fair ;
I shall worship Thee for ever
  In Thy glory there.

G. TER STEEGEN, † 1769.

E

THE BELOVED

"He is altogether lovely."—CANT. v. 16.

O DEW abundant from the depths divine,
O sweet white Flower, pure as mountain
    snow,
O precious Fruit of that celestial Flower,
O Ransom from the everlasting woe—
Thou holy sacrifice for sins of men,
The gift that the eternal Father gave—
O Dew of life, by Thee I live again,
By Thee Who camest down to seek and
    save.
I see Thee small in low and humble guise,
And me Thou seest, great in shame and
    sin—
Lord, I would be Thy daily sacrifice,
Though I am worthless, vile, and foul
    within.
Yet into that mean cup Thy grace will
    pour
The love that overflows for evermore.

            MECHTHILD OF HELLFDE, † 1277.

THE LAMB OF GOD

"A Lamb without blemish and without spot."
—1 PET. i. 19.

LAMB, Thy white-robed people feeding
   'Neath the shadowing wings—
Lamb, Thy weary, thirsty leading,
   To the living springs.
Once upon the altar bleeding,
   Now on God's high throne—
Unto Thee salvation, glory,
   Lamb of God, alone.
We before the throne in Heaven
   Day and night adore
Thee, the Lamb, amongst us dwelling
   Now, and evermore !
Lo, we hunger not and thirst not,
   Nor can sun or heat
Smite us in Thy rest and shadow
   Deep, and still, and sweet.
Days and nights of lonely sorrow.
   Long and changeful years,
Tell but of the Hand most tender,
   Wiping all our tears.

For our robes, so white, so radiant,
Witness as they shine
Of the Sacred Blood that washed us,
Thine, O Lamb Divine.

T. S. M.

THE GREAT UNKNOWN

"I have called, and ye refused; I have stretched out
My hand, and no man regarded."—PROV. i. 24.

"There standeth One among you, whom ye know
not."—JOHN i. 26.

WHY dost Thou pass unheeded,
Treading with piercèd feet
The halls of the kingly palace,
The busy street?
Oh marvellous in Thy beauty,
Crowned with the light of God,
Why fall they not down to worship
Where Thou has trod?
Why are Thy hands extended
Beseeching whilst men pass by
With their empty words and their laughter,
Yet passing on to die?

Unseen, unknown, unregarded,
  Calling and waiting yet—
They hear Thy knock and they tremble—
  They hear, and they forget.
And Thou in the midst art standing
  Of old and for ever the same—
Thou hearest their songs and their jesting,
    But not Thy Name.
The thirty-three years forgotten
  Of the weary way Thou hast trod—
Thou art but a name unwelcome,
    O Saviour God !
Yet amongst the highways and hedges,
  Amongst the lame and the blind,
The poor and the maimed and the outcast,
  Still dost Thou seek and find—
There by the wayside lying
  The eyes of Thy love can see
The wounded, the naked, the dying,
  Too helpless to come to Thee.
So art Thou watching and waiting
  Till the wedding is furnished with guests—
And the last of the sorrowful singeth,
  And the last of the weary rests.

C. P. O.

TRANSFORMED

"I send thee to open their eyes, and to turn them
from darkness to light, and from the power of
Satan unto God, that they may receive forgiveness of sins, and inheritance among them which are
sanctified by faith that is in Me."—Acts xxvi. 18.

Dark lay the plain, a tangled wilderness,
And dark the mountains in the mists
 afar—
A land of darkness where no order is,
 Nor moon, nor star—
There was the line of drear confusion drawn,
The stones of emptiness lay wide and
 bare,
As though the ancient peoples of the dawn
 Lay buried there.
There did the wild beasts of the desert
 meet
The creatures from the waste and lonely
 isles—
And there did nameless shadows glide and
 fleet
 Through ruined piles.

There in the mouldered palaces there spread
The nettles, and the brambles and the
   thorn ;
Now and again there brake the silence dread
   Some cry forlorn.
And now and yet again a pallid light,
A magic gleam from out the darkness
   shone—
And then into a deeper, drearier night
   It wandered on.
And he who dwells there dwelleth all alone,
All unaware of those who wander by ;
They unto him, and he to them unknown,
   They live and die.
Know'st thou the land ? the land where
   wandered first
The two who could remember Paradise—
The land of hunger, and of quenchless thirst,
   Of tear-worn eyes.
Know'st thou the land ? too early known
   —too well,
Though veiled awhile in childhood's golden
   haze ;
But bare and drear when past the song and
   spell,
   The infant days.

Thy land, O soul, thy fatherland of old—
The far, far country thou didst choose for
    thee;
Choose, rather than the palaces of gold,
    Where God must be.

.   .   .   .   .

The wilderness, the solitary place,
    No more are sad—
Are lit with radiance of His glorious Face—
    The wastes are glad ;
They blossom as the roses thousand-fold,
    They sing and they rejoice ;
The glory of the mighty cedars old,
    The summer's voice,
The fresh green pastures, and the waters still
    From fountains fed,
Where far aloft upon God's holy hill
    The Angels tread—
These, where the ancient land of darkness lay,
    Lie still and fair ;
The eyes unsealed to that eternal Day
    Behold Him there.
Amidst the wilderness the waters flow,
    The streams for ever spring ;
Beside them in their raiment white as snow
    The ransomed sing.

They pass along with music and with song,
  And joy their diadem—
To God's fair city wends the glorious throng,
  And Jesus walks with them.
Know'st thou the Way? the one Highway
  of God
  That leads therein?
The pathway of the Lamb's most precious
  blood
  Who bore thy sin?
Know'st thou the Way? the glorious Way
  He made
  Through death's deep sea?
O Lamb of God, I bless the love that laid
  My sins on Thee.

C. P. C.

LIGHT AND SOUND

"Then the eyes of the blind shall be opened, and the
ears of the deaf shall be unstopped."—Is. xxxv. 5.

THOU glorious Lord! mine eyes at last un-
  sealed
  Behold Thee now—
In sudden radiance to my soul revealed,
  Light, sight, art Thou.

One moment—and the night has passed
    away,
Unbarred the prison ;
And I pass forth to God's eternal day,
    The dead arisen.
One moment—and I see Thy glorious Face
    Look down on me,
Unutterable love that fills all space,
    Where'er I be.
Here, nearer than myself, and far away
    And everywhere,
Thou shinest, Light of that celestial day,
    "The Lord is there."
Thou showest me the land of living springs,
    The land that lies
Beneath the shadow of Thy mighty wings,
    The glory of Thine eyes.
And all is lit with love that hath no end,
    Illimitable love—
Wherein for ever wheresoe'er I wend
    I live and move.
Such, O my God, that moment of delight—
    The sudden light that shone
Upon the fields of Bethlehem at night—
    Thou givest me Thy Son.

       .   .   .   .

And now the silence of the dead is past;
My ears have heard
The voice of Him who is the First and Last,
The living Word.
But not in one short moment hath He
told
His heart to me,
The everlasting love that was of old,
That evermore shall be.
My ears have heard the first entrancing
chord
Of that unending song,
The joyful psalm, the music of the Lord,*
So sweet, so long.
The song that through the everlasting
days
The Lord's belovèd hears;
His Light has filled illimitable space,
His Voice, eternal years.
O glorious moment of the opened eyes,
Himself revealed!
O endless years of songs of Paradise
For ears unsealed!

C. P. C.

* 2 Chron. vii. 6.

TO-MORROW

"There remaineth therefore a rest to the people ot
God."—HEB. iv. 9.

THERE is a Day of rest before thee—
Thou weary soul, arise and shine.
Awhile the clouds hung darkly o'er thee,
    Awhile the captive's chains were thine.
Behold, the Lamb of God will lead thee
    To still green pastures round the throne ;
Cast off thy burden, rise and speed thee,
    For soon the battle storm is done—
For soon the weary race is past,
And thou shalt rest in Love at last.

God 'stablished ere the days of Heaven
    Rest, gentle rest, for evermore—
Men long have wept, and toiled, and striven,
    But rest was ordered long before,
For this the Saviour left the skies,
    The Home beyond the thousand suns—
He stretches forth His hands and cries,
    "Come, come to Me, ye weary ones !
Ye long have laboured, come and rest,
Lie still, belovèd, on My breast.

Then come, ye sorrowful and weary.
  Ye heavy laden, come to Him,
From desert places lone and dreary,
  With fainting heart and aching limb;
For ye have borne the heat of day,
  And now the hour of rest is come;
To you the Lord doth call and say,
  "My people, I will be your Home;
Fear not for devil, world, and sin,
But saved and pardoned, enter in."

Come in, the sheaves of glory bringing,
  The seed-time of our tears is past,
More sweet than dreams of joy the singing
  That fills our Father's house at last.
And grief and fear, and death and pain,
  Are fled, and are forgotten things;
We see the Lamb that once was slain,
  He leads us to the living springs;
Himself He wipes our tears away—
Such blessedness words cannot say.

The day of deep refreshing dawneth;
  No sun lights on us, and no heat;
No longer is there one who mourneth,
  And there the hearts long severed meet—

And God Himself shall be with them ;
They who the weary desert trod,
Shall be a royal Diadem
    For ever in the Hand of God ;
All hail I thou glorious Sabbath day
When toil and strife are past away!

And peace is round us as a river,
    And glory as a flowing stream ;
With Christ our Lord we dwell for ever,
    For ever lean in love on Him.
Oh give me wings to flee away
    Afar into that holy home !
Why seek we still on earth to stay ?
    The Spirit and the Bride say "Come !"
Arise ! Salvation draweth near
The everlasting Sabbath year.

                              J. S. KUNTH, † 1700.

THE BREATH OF GOD

"The wind bloweth where it listeth, and thou hearest
the sound thereof."—JOHN iii. 8.

THOU Breath from still eternity
Breathe o'er my spirit's barren land—
The pine-tree and the myrtle-tree
Shall spring amidst the desert sand ;
And where Thy living water flows
The waste shall blossom as the rose.

May I in will and deed and word
Obey Thee as a little child ;
And keep me in Thy love, my Lord,
For ever holy, undefiled ;
Within me teach, and strive, and pray,
Lest I should choose my own wild way.

O Spirit, Stream that by the Son
Is opened to us crystal pure,
Forth flowing from the heavenly Throne
To waiting hearts and spirits poor,
Athirst and weary do I sink
Beside Thy waters, there to drink.

My spirit turns to Thee and clings,
　All else forsaking, unto Thee;
Forgetting all created things,
　Remembering only "God in me."
O living Stream; O gracious rain,
None wait for Thee, and wait in vain.

　　　　　　　G. TER STEEGEN, † 1769.

THE WILL OF GOD

"Here am I, let Him do to me as seemeth good
unto Him."—2 SAM. xv. 26.

THOU sweet beloved Will of God,
　My anchor ground, my fortress hill,
The Spirit's silent fair abode,
　In Thee I hide me and am still.

O Will, that willest good alone,
　Lead Thou the way, Thou guidest best;
A silent child, I follow on,
　And trusting, lean upon Thy Breast.

God's Will doth make the bitter sweet,
　And all is well when it is done;
Unless His Will doth hallow it,
　The glory of all joy is gone.

Self, Sense, and Reason, they may scorn
　That hidden way that leads on high—
Still be my deepest will uptorn,
　And so the power of Nature die.

And if in gloom I see Thee not,
　I lean upon Thy love unknown—
In me Thy blessed Will is wrought,
　If I will nothing of my own.

O spirit of a little child,
　Of will bereft, untroubled, pure,
I seek thy glory undefiled ;
　Lord, take my will, Thy love is sure.

O Will of God, my soul's desire,
　My Bread of life in want and pain ;
O Will of God, my guiding fire,
　Unite my will to Thine again.

O Will, in me Thy work be done,
For time, and for eternity—
Give joy or sorrow, all are one
To that blest soul that loveth Thee.

G. Ter Steegen.

THE VICTORY OF THE LAMB

"If we suffer, we shall also reign with Him."
—2 Tim. ii. 12.

I go from grief and sighing, the valley and
the clod,
To join the chosen people in the palaces of
God—
There sounds no cry of battle amidst the
shadowing palms,
But the mighty song of victory, and glorious
golden psalms.

The army of the conquerors, a palm in every
hand,
In robes of state and splendour, in rest
eternal stand ;

Those marriage robes of glory, the righteousness of God—
He bought them for His people with His
most precious Blood.

The Lamb of God has saved them from Hell's
deep sea of fire—
The Lamb of God adorns them in spotless
white attire;
The Lamb of God presents them as Kings in
crowns of light—
As Priests in God's own temple to serve Him
day and night.

Salvation, strength, and wisdom to Him whose
works and ways
Are wonderful and glorious—eternal is His
praise :
The Lamb Who died and liveth, alive for
evermore,
The Saviour Who redeemed us, for ever we
adore.

J. HEERMAN, † 1647.

THE CITY THAT HATH FOUNDATIONS

"I . . . saw the Holy City, New Jerusalem."
—REV. xxi. 2.

JERUSALEM! thou glorious City-height,
　　Oh might I enter in!
My spirit wearieth for thy love and light,
　　Amidst this world of sin—
Far over the dark mountains,
　　The moorlands cold and grey,
She looketh with sad longing,
　　And fain would flee away.

O fair sweet day! and hour yet more fair
　　When wilt thou come to me?
My spirit, safe within my Saviour's care
　　Made glad, and pure, and free—
And calmly, surely trusting
　　His faithful loving Hand
Shall she be led in safety
　　To Heaven, her Fatherland.

One moment! Ere she is aware, she treads
    The glorious shore that lies
Beyond the stars, beyond the midnight
    shades,
    Beyond the stormy skies,—
The chariot of Elijah,
    The shining angel throng
Shall bear her through the Heavens,
    With triumph and with song.

O City beautiful! Thy light appears—
    The gates by grace set wide—
The Home for which through long, long
    exile years,
    My weary spirit sighed—
The false and empty shadows,
    The life of sin, are past—
God gives me mine inheritance,
    The land of life at last.

But who are they that come—the glorious
    ones,
    As stars along the way—
A royal diadem of pleasant stones?
    My Lord's elect are they:

He sent them forth to meet me,
　　Where dark with mist of fears,
The land of gloom lay round me,
　　My distant land of tears.

The Patriarchs and Saints of olden days,
　　The Christians all unknown,
Who bore the heat of persecution blaze,
　　Or nameless Cross alone—
I see them crowned with glory,
　　And shining from afar ;
To them the Lord their Saviour,
　　Has given the Morning-Star.

Oh when at last I reach that City fair,
　　That beauteous Paradise,
To sing unto the Love that led me there,
　　Eternal melodies,
Then only can I give Thee
　　The praises that are meet,
With Hallelujah thunder,
　　With psaltery clear and sweet.

Before the emerald encircled throne,
　　The thousand choirs fall ;
Their song of praises echoing ever on
　　Through Heaven's high palace hall.

The throng that none can number,
Of every race and tongue,
Join like the mighty waters
In that eternal Song.

J. M. MEYFART, † 1642.

THE WELCOME

"This man receiveth sinners, and eateth with them."
—LUKE xv. 2.

SINNERS Jesus will receive—
Say this word of grace to all
Who the heavenly pathway leave,
All who linger, all who fall !—
This can bring them back again,
Christ receiveth sinful men.

Shepherds seek their wandering sheep
O'er the mountains bleak and cold—
Jesus such a watch doth keep
O'er the lost ones of His fold—
Seeking them o'er moor and fen ;
Christ receiveth sinful men.

Come, and He will give you rest;
 Sorrow stricken, sin defiled—
He can make the sinfullest
 God the Father's blessed child;
Trust Him, for His word is plain,
Christ receiveth sinful men.

Sick, and sorrowful, and blind,
 I with all my sins draw nigh;
O my Saviour, Thou canst find
 Help for sinners such as I.
Speak that word of love again,
Christ receiveth sinful men.

Yea, my soul is comforted,
 For Thy Blood hath washed away
All my sins though crimson red,
 And I stand in white array—
Purged from every spot and stain—
Christ receiveth sinful men.

Now my heart condemns me not,
 Pure before the Law I stand;
He who cleansed me from all spot
 Satisfied its last demand;
Who shall dare accuse me then?
Christ receiveth sinful men.

Christ receiveth sinful men—
Even me with all my sin ;
Openeth to me Heaven again,
With Him I may enter in.
Death hath no more sting nor pain,
Christ receiveth sinful men.

E. NEUMEISTER, † 1756.

THY HIDDEN ONES

"The world knoweth us not, because it knew Him
not."—1 JOHN iii. 1.

ALL fair within those Children of the
    light,
Though dark their brows beneath the desert
    sun ;
Mysterious joys, far hidden from all sight,
The King of Glory giveth to each one—
    No thought of man has pictured them,
    No hand may touch that diadem ;
    Within God's light His own abide
    With hidden glory glorified.

To earthly eyes they are as Adam's race—
They wear the earthly form, and scars of
pain,
On them as on all sinners leave their trace;
Their outward needs are those of other men.
And theirs the forms of earthly life,
Theirs sleeping, waking, want, and strife,
Yet this they have that they despise
What fairest seems to earthly eyes.

And inwardly their life is from above,
The Lord's Almighty Word hath quick-
ened them;
Flames kindled from the everlasting Love,
The children of the New Jerusalem;
Their brethren are the Saints in light,
And songs of sweetness infinite
They sing with them to God Most High,
A deep and wondrous melody.

They walk upon the earth, and dwell in
Heaven,
Though powerless, guard the world with
arms unseen;
Deep peace to them in midst of strife is given,
And all they wish they have, though poor
and mean.

Storms beat them, but may not destroy,
Fast rooted in eternal joy;
They walk as in the shade of death,
Yet living on in silent faith.

When Christ their Life shall be made mani-
fest,
When He shall come with all His power to
rule,
Their glory, hidden long, shall be con-
fessed;
Arise and shine ! O bright and beautiful !
With Christ ye shall ascend on high,
Victorious in His victory—
The hidden light shall shine afar,
Each saint an everlasting star.

Rejoice, thou Earth ! Be glad, O field and
hill,
That ye are for a little while their home ;
The Lord Jehovah thus doth set His seal
In token of His blessing yet to come.
And when to make His diadem
He bringeth forth each hidden gem,
He then shall hear thy weary sighs,
The earth shall be as Paradise.

Thou hidden Life of faithful souls—Thou
    Light
Of that mysterious inner world of thought,
Oh give us grace to follow Thee aright,
From cross and toil and sorrow shrinking
    not;
  Content to be but little known,
  Content to wander on alone;
  Here—hidden inwardly in Thee ;
  There—Light in thine own Light to be.

C. F. Richter, † 1711.

THE BLESSED HOPE

"Faultless before the presence of His glory."
—Jude 24.

In faith we sing this song of thankfulness
  For that deep comfort Christ's belovèd
    share ;
The blessed Hope of everlasting peace,
  The Home in God's high glory bright and
    fair;
Awhile we wander in the wilderness,
  But that eternal Home awaits us there.

True is it that no heart may comprehend
  The glory God prepareth for His own,
And what will happen when this age shall
    end ;
But yet in vision Jesus hath made known
How fair and holy shall His Church descend,
  Lit up with light of precious jasper stone.

And He shall give her honour in that day,
  For unto Him all power and might are
    given ;
In soul and body, freed from earth's decay,
  Her mortal semblance purified and shriven,
Shall she put on her beautiful array
  Of new eternal Life, He brought from
    Heaven.

And Heaven and Earth, and all created
    things,
  In wondrous beauty then shall be re-
    stored ;
And we shall rest from all our wanderings,
  Partakers of the nature of our Lord,
And made to God our Father priests and
    kings,
  In light whereto the Angels never soared.

And He shall make His Church all heavenly
   fair,
   With gold and pearls, and every radiant
   stone,
And reign in Holiness and Glory there,
   And shine as suns and stars have never
   shone;
And He shall lead His Bride, His Joy and
   Care,
   With blissful singing to His Father's throne.

With eyes undimmed shall she her God be-
   hold,
   Behold Him face to face, and walk by sight,
Not trusting only, as in days of old,
   But seeing with her eyes eternal Light.
The great Salvation mystery shall unfold
   In that high vision of Love infinite.

And then the Saints shall rest in victory,
   Their weary battle-day is at an end;
Amidst the Holy Angels joy shall be,
   That we and they can love as friend and
   friend;
We weep no more, for one with Christ are we,
   In oneness love alone may comprehend.

And then shall be the blest Communion,
  Of God's dear children meeting from
    afar;
Within His burning Love they blend as
    one,
  Yet each, according as His counsels are,
Shall have peculiar glory of his own,
  As one star differeth from another star.

And God is all in all in that great day,
  And He is their exceeding great Reward;
Their stream of Life, their beautiful array,
  Their food, their joy, their radiance, Christ
    the Lord:
The music of their wondrous song shall say,
  How great the joy that passeth thought
    or word.

And this is that eternal life of Heaven,
  Laid up with Christ in God, the mystery
Of Resurrection Life which He hath given:
  A Fount of living waters full and free;
A Life by which the gates of death are
    riven,
  A Life which on the throne of Christ
    shall be.

And here in this waste wilderness begun,
    So soon as we believe in Christ aright,
And quickened by the Spirit of the Son,
    Receive Him as our only Life and Light,
As all the branches in the Vine are one,
    So we are one for ever in His sight.

Now come Thou quickly, Jesus, from above.
    Do Thou sustain us on the desert road,
And draw us after Thee by might of love,
    Our Fatherland art Thou, O Love of God :
Once safe in Thee, no more shall we remove,
    O Thou our everlasting sure abode.

MORAVIAN BRETHREN.

MY HIGH TOWER

"He only is my rock and my salvation: He is my
defence, I shall not be moved."—Ps. lxii. 6.

Is God for me? I fear not, though all
    against me rise ;
I call on Christ my Saviour, the host of evil
    flies.

My friend the Lord Almighty, and He who
    loves me, God,
What enemy shall harm me, though coming
    as a flood?
I know it, I believe it, I say it fear-
    lessly,
That God, the Highest, Mightiest, for ever
    loveth me;
At all times, in all places, He standeth at
    my side,
He rules the battle fury, the tempest and
    the tide.

A Rock that stands for ever is Christ my
    Righteousness,
And there I stand unfearing in everlasting
    bliss;
No earthly thing is needful to this my life
    from Heaven,
And nought of love is worthy, save that
    which Christ has given.
Christ, all my praise and glory, my Light
    most sweet and fair,
The ship wherein He saileth is scatheless
    everywhere;

In Him I dare be joyful, a hero in the
war,
The judgment of the sinner affrighteth me
no more.

There is no condemnation, there is no hell
for me,
The torment and the fire my eyes shall never
see ;
For me there is no sentence, for me has death
no stings,
Because the Lord Who saved me shall shield
me with His wings.
Above my soul's dark waters His Spirit
hovers still,
He guards me from all sorrow, from terror
and from ill ;
In me He works and blesses the life-seed He
has sown,
From Him I learn the Abba, that prayer of
faith alone.

And if in lonely places, a fearful child, I
shrink,
He prays the prayers within me I cannot ask
or think ;

In deep unspoken language, known only to
that Love
Who fathoms the heart's mystery from the
Throne of Light above.
His Spirit to my spirit sweet words of com-
fort saith,
How God the weak one strengthens who
leans on Him in faith;
How He hath built a City, of love, and light,
and song,
Where the eye at last beholdeth what the
heart had loved so long.

And there is mine inheritance, my kingly
palace-home;
The leaf may fall and perish, not less the
spring will come ;
As wind and rain of winter, our earthly sighs
and tears,
Till the golden summer dawneth of the end-
less Year of years.
The world may pass and perish, Thou, God,
wilt not remove—
No hatred of all devils can part me from
Thy Love;

No hungering nor thirsting, no poverty nor
　　care,
No wrath of mighty princes can reach my
　　shelter there.

No Angel, and no Heaven, no throne, nor
　　power, nor might,
No love, no tribulation, no danger, fear, nor
　　fight,
No height, no depth, no creature that has
　　been or can be,
Can drive me from Thy bosom, can sever me
　　from Thee.
My heart in joy upleapeth, grief cannot linger
　　there—
While singing high in glory amidst the sun-
　　shine fair ;
The source of all my singing is high in
　　Heaven above ;
The Sun that shines upon me is Jesus and
　　His Love.

PAUL GERHARDT, † 1676.

THE LAND OF PROMISE

'All the Land which thou seest, to thee will I give it.'
—GEN. xiii. 15.

IT was as if upon His breast
  He laid His piercèd hand,
And said "To thee, beloved and blest,
  I give this goodly land."

O Land of fountains and of deeps,
  Of God's exhaustless store—
O blessed Land, where he who reaps
  Shall never hunger more—

O summer Land, for ever fair
  With God's unfading flowers ;
O Land, where spices fill the air,
  And songs the golden towers—

O Land of safety, Land of home,
  Of God my Father's kiss,
To Thee, O glorious Land, I come,
  My heritage of bliss.

Lord, not through works of righteousness,
The works that I have done,
But through the glory of Thy grace,
The merit of Thy Son,

To me this goodly Land is given,
The heart of Christ to me—
My Home, my Blessedness, my Heaven;
My God, I worship Thee.

GERTRUDE OF HELLFDE, † 1330.

THE FRIEND

"We will come unto him, and make Our abode
with him."—JOHN xiv. 23.

IT thus befell me on a day
When gladsome was the month of May,
I sat alone in pleasant thought
Beside the fish-pond in the court;
Above me spread the lindens tall,
And deep-blue heavens were over all,
How dear is that old court to me!
So sunny, still, and fair to see—

The water flowing clear and bright,
And many a tree with blossoms dight,
And singing birds, and doves that fly
All white across the summer sky ,
And there, of all delights the best,
The blessed stillness and the rest.

Then thought I, " All is fair and sweet—
What need I more in my retreat,
In sooth that this still hour may be
As dew from Heaven that falls on me ?
So were it, if there came from Heaven
   A faithful friend and dear,
Whose words should be a dew to me
   Of comfort and of cheer.
Then I should grow as lilies sweet
   That in God's garden are,
Whose strange and wondrous odours
   greet
Some wandering soul afar."

Then answered, ere I was aware,
   The Voice beloved and true—
The blessed Friend from Heaven was
   there,
   My Sunshine and my Dew ;

The Fountain for the souls that thirst,
 The cup that runneth o'er—
The Lord Who gives the longing first,
 Then stills it evermore—

He told me of the River bright
 That flows from Him to me,
That I might be for His delight
 A fair and fruitful tree.

He told me that as doves that rise
 Far through the golden light,
So He would lead me through the skies
 In raiment pure and white.

That as the still fair court to me
 Afar from strife and din,
So unto Him my heart should be,
 And He would rest therein.

And when the evening shadows fell,
And all was silent in my cell,
And on my knees I knelt and prayed
To Him Who is my Sun and Shade,
There came to me that saying deep,
" Who loveth Me, My words will keep.

And him My Father loveth well,
And We will come with him to dwell."
Yea, Lord, through Thy most precious Blood,
Am I the resting-place of God.

GERTRUDE OF HELLFDE, † 1330.

MORE THAN HEAVEN

" A throne was set in Heaven, and One sat on the
throne."—REV. iv. 2.

JESUS, Lord, in Whom the Father
    Tells His heart to me—
Jesus, God Who made the Heavens,
    Made the earth to be—

Jesus, Lamb of God once offered
    For the guilt of men,
In the Heavens interceding
    Till Thou come again—

Jesus, once by God abandoned,
    Smitten, cursed for me,
Sentenced at the throne of judgment,
    Dying on the tree—

Jesus, risen and ascended,
On the Father's throne,
All the Heaven of Heavens resounding
With Thy Name alone—

There, beholding Thee, forgetting
Sorrow, sin, and care,
Know I not that earth is darkened;
Nor that Heaven is fair—

Songs and psalteries of Heaven
Hushed the while I hear
Thy beloved Voice that speaketh,
Sweet, and still, and near;

That entrancing Song that ever
Thou shalt sing alone—
Joy that Thou hast sought and found me,
Won me for Thine own.

Barred to me that Heavenly Eden
Till the flaming Sword,
In God's righteous wrath uplifted,
Smote Thee, O my Lord.

Led within those gates unguarded,
　Paradise is mine ;
But the glory and the beauty
　Is that love of Thine.

Therefore, O my Lord, I reckon
　All things else as loss ;
More than Heaven itself is precious,
　Memory of Thy Cross.

More than Heaven itself Thou givest
　In the desert now,
For the crown of my rejoicing,
　Jesus, Lord, art Thou.

C. P. C.

TWILIGHT

"Abide with us : for it is toward evening, and the day
　is far spent."—LUKE xxiv. 29.

THE day is gone—my soul looks on
　To that eternal Day,
When all our sorrow, all our sin,
　Have fled and passed away.

The golden sun is sunk and gone,
  Thou Light of Heaven above,
Thou Glory of eternal day,
  My sunshine is Thy love.

Each living thing lies slumbering
  From care and labour free ;
May I, O Lord, be still and watch
  Thy hidden work in me.

But when shall cease the changefulness
  Of morning and of night?
Then when the Glory of the Lord
  Is our eternal Light.

No cloud shall come, no evening gloom
  On Salem shall descend ;
The Lord her everlasting Day,
  Her mourning at an end.

All praise to Thee! Oh there to be
  Amidst that music-flood!
The many waters echoing round
  The golden shores of God.

O Jesus mine, Thou Rest divine,
Lead me to Zion's height,
Where I, with all Thy ransomed ones,
Shall walk with Thee in white.

J. A. FREYLINGHAUSEN, † 1739.

ANCHORED

"An Anchor of the soul, both sure and stedfast."
—HEB. vi. 19.

MY soul hath found the steadfast ground,
There ever shall my anchor hold—
That ground is in my Saviour Christ,
Before the world was from of old—
And that sure ground shall be my stay,
When Heaven and Earth shall pass away.

That ground is Thine Eternal Love,
Thy Love that through all ages burns—
The open arms of mercy stretched
To meet the sinner who returns;
The Love that calleth everywhere,
If men will hear or will forbear.

God willeth not we should be lost,
  He wills to save the sons of men ;
For this His Son came down from Heaven,
  For this returned to Heaven again ;
For this He standeth at the door,
He knocketh, waiteth, evermore—

Unseen, unheard, He calleth yet ;
  Rejected, still He waits to bless—
The Shepherd never will forget
  His lost sheep in the wilderness ;
Though far as east from west they stray,
He seeketh them by night and day.

O deep, deep sea, where all our sins
  By God are cast, and found no more !
There is no condemnation now,
  The Lord hath healed our deadly sore ;
Because the voice of Jesu's Blood
Still cries for mercy unto God.

In that deep sea of love I sink
  In perfect peace and endless rest,
And when my sins condemn my soul,
  Cling closer to my Saviour's breast—
For there I find, go when I will,
Unchanging love and mercy still.

J. A. ROTHE, † 1758.

THE EVERLASTING ARMS

"His left hand is under my head, and His right hand
doth embrace me."—CANT. ii. 6.

WEARILY my spirit sinketh
Into Jesu's Heart and Hands,
Calmly trusting, though the journey
　Lie through strange untrodden lands.
All my spirit is at rest
On the loving Father's breast.

There my spirit cannot murmur,
　Pleased with all that may betide—
What the will of Self would cherish
　Is already crucified—
Buried is each murmuring word
In the grave of Christ my Lord.

There my spirit cannot question,
　Little doth she think or say;
All the thorns of life around her
　Cannot take her peace away—
He who made me guideth best,
And my heart is left at rest.

There my spirit knows no darkness,
　Love remains when all is gone—
Sorrows crushing soul and body
　Do the heathens know alone—
Resting in Christ's blessed light,
Fears she not the earthly night.

There my spirit is not careful,
　For she knoweth of no ill ;
Hanging still upon her Father,
　Though He slay her, trusting still ;
How shall flesh and blood repine
Where the chastening is divine ?

Thus on God my spirit waiteth,
　Even so doth overcome ;
Silently enduring all things,
　Mockery and martyrdom ;
Like a still sea doth she lie,
Full of praise to God most high.

J. J. WINKLER, † 1722.

THINGS TO COME

"He will show you things to come."—John xvi. 13.

On what will be the day when won at last
    The last long weary battle, we shall come
To those eternal gates the King hath passed,
    Returning from our exile to our Home ;
When earth's last dust is washed from off
      our feet ;
The last sweat from our brows is wiped
      away ;
The hopes that made our pilgrim journey
      sweet
    All met around us, realised that day !

Oh what will be the day, when we shall stand
    Irradiate with God's eternal light ;
First tread as sinless saints the sinless land,
    No shade nor stain upon our garments
      white ;
No fear, no shame upon our faces then,
    No mark of sin—oh joy beyond all thought !
A son of God, a free-born citizen
    Of that bright city where the curse is not !

H

Oh what will be the day when with our
    prayer
Eternal singing shall be woven in—
Deep sound of golden harps far echoing
    there
    To praise the Lamb who took away our
    sin ;
When far and wide the radiant streets
    resound
    With Hallelujah songs the ransomed sing,
And clouds of sweetest incense rise around
    The Throne where sits in light the Saviour
    King !

Oh what will be the day when we shall see
    The Love that opened Heaven to ransomed
    men !
Love draws us and we follow—we are free—
    Nought severs us from our Belovèd then :
That veil of faith through which we looked
    of old
    Has passed away as mist before the sun ;
Christ throned in glory do our eyes behold,
    O'er worlds, through ages, reigning ever
    on.

Oh what will be the day when we shall hear
"Come, oh ye blessed !" when we take our
place
Before His throne in radiance sweet and
clear,
Behold His glorious, His belovèd Face—
Behold the Eyes whence bitter tears have
flowed
For all our grief, our hardness, and our sin—
Behold the wounds whence streamed the
precious Blood,
Which ransomed us, and washed us pure
and clean !

Oh what will be the day when hand in hand,
Saints wander through the pastures green
and fair,
The trees of life upon the golden strand
As fresh as on the third day morn are
there ;
There all is new, and never shall be old,
For time is not, nor age, nor slow decay ;
No dying eyes, no hearts grown strange and
cold,
All pain, all death, all sighing fled away !

Oh what will be the day when every thought
   Of that dark valley we have left below,
And all remembrance of the fight we fought,
   Our pilgrim journey, long and sad, and
      slow,
Shall only make the Glory brighter far,
   Shall make the peace but deeper, sweeter
      yet?
O'er that dark sea was Christ our Guiding
      Star,
Our love were fainter love could we forget.

Oh what will be that day? no eye can see,
   No ear can hear, no heart has yet con-
      ceived,
What God shall give us, and what we shall
      be
When we inherit what we have believed.
O Land of Promise! rough may be the
      road,
   And long the race may be—but sweet the
      end;
The dead with Christ, the risen sons of God,
   With Him we journey, and with Him
      ascend.

SPITTA, 1800.

A NEW SONG

"He hath put a new song in my mouth, even praise
unto our God."—Ps. xl. 3.

I KNOW not the song of Thy praises,
    Till Thou teach it, my God, to me—
Till I hear the still voice of Thy Spirit,
    Who speaketh for ever of Thee—
Till I hear the celestial singing,
    And learn the new song of Thy grace,
And then shall I tell forth the marvels
    I learnt in Thy secret place.
Thy marvels, not mine, far surpassing
    All thoughts of my heart must they be—
I can but declare the glad tidings,
    As Thou hast declared them to me.

R. ROLLE, † 1349.

THE COURTS OF GOD

"Lord, I have loved the habitation of Thy house,
and the place where Thine honour dwelleth."
—Ps. xxvi. 8.

O Lord, I have loved the fair beauty
Of the house Thou hast chosen for Thee,
The courts where Thy gladness rejoiceth,
And where Thou delightest to be.
For I love to be made the fair dwelling
Where God in His grace may abide ;
I would cast forth whatever may grieve
Thee,
And welcome none other beside.
Oh blessed the grace that has made me
The home of the gladness of God,
The dwelling wherein Thou delightest,
The house Thou hast bought with Thy
blood.
'Tis there that Thy joy overfloweth,
I feel it, I take of it there ;
By the work that Thou workest within me,
The temple is holy and fair.

In the secret of that inner chamber,
    Is Thy settle of heavenly rest ;
The stillness of thoughts that adore Thee,
    The shrine that Thou lovest the best.
The temple where Christ hath His dwelling,
    The soul He hath ransomed and shriven—
The temple where I have my dwelling,
    Is Christ in the glory of Heaven.

                        R. ROLLE, † 1349.

A SONG OF THE TEMPLE

"In His Temple doth every one speak of His glory."
                —Ps. xxix. 9.

IN Thy tabernacle, Lord, I offer
    Sacrifice of psalmody and song—
Thine uncounted mercies there recalling,
    Praising Thee with music sweet and
        strong.

With a marvellous, a mighty gladness,
    For the love of Christ is shed abroad
In the soul that is His holy temple,
    And she singeth therefore unto God.

She ascends aloft to join the singing,
Heard afar from God's Jerusalem—*
Blessed music of the saints she heareth,
And adoring singeth she with them.

None can know though skilled in learning
    ancient,
What the sweetness of that song may be ;
Till he know the glory and the gladness,
There the blessed Face of God to see.

Lord, to Thee my heart is ever yearning,
    In this absence seeking still Thy Face ;
Blessed hour when I shall find !—adoring
    In the glory of Thy holy place !

                              R. ROLLE, † 1349.

* Neh. xii. 43.

FOR THE CHILDREN

PREFACE

Everywhere, everywhere,
   A tale is told to me—
It is told in the sunny air,
   It is told on the sparkling sea ;

It is told in the forest brakes,
   It is told on the purple hills,
By the silent mountain lakes,
   By the singing and leaping rills.

In the ancient gardens grand,
   With their old-world flowers aglow,
Where the stately cedars stand,
   And the sweet limes all a-row.

In the meadows that stretch away
   As a sea of golden green,
With hedges of sweet white may
   And the reedy brooks between.

Where I wander, and run, and rest,
   The tale is told to me,
The sweetest tale and the best
   Of all the tales that be.

.   .   .   .

The tale is the tale of Jesus—
It is told in Heaven above,
On the sea and the moors and the mountains,
In language of all the peoples,
The speech of love.

The morning star and the dayspring,
The sun and the cloud and the shower,
The grass and the rose and the cedar,
His glory and love are telling
From hour to hour.

The birds in the greenwood singing,
The sea that is deep and wide,
The sheep in the folds of the mountains,
The corn in the golden valleys,
And all beside.

All round me the glorious pictures
Of Him who has made them fair ;
Through the long bright day I can see Him,
And I fear not the silent darkness,
For He is there.

COME forth in the fields and the gardens ;
  There let us seek and find
All that will tell us of Jesus,
  And bring His love to mind.
All white on the thymy hillside
  Lambs by their mothers play ;
All white stand the stately lilies
  In the garden borders gay.
All white in the sunny heavens
  The piled-up clouds sail slow—
They were crimson when rose the morning.
  Now whiter are they than snow,
All white on the lonely mountains
  The snow where no foot has trod—
All white is the foam on the fountains
  That flow from the hills of God.

Oh tell me what yet is whiter
  Than the lambs and the lilies white,
Than the clouds piled up in the noontide,
  Like a mountain land of light ?

Than the snow on the ancient mountains,
  Where only the angels go?
Than the foam where the wild bright
    fountains
  Dance down to the glens below?

Child, hast thou trusted Jesus?
  Canst thou believe and say,
" He loved me, He died to save me,
  He has borne my sins away;
For my sins were laid upon Jesus;
  In my stead, for my guilt, He died"?
Then child, fall down and adore Him,
  Thou art whiter than all beside.
A lamb washed white for ever
  In the Lamb's most precious blood—
A lily by God's still river,
  That lies in the light of God.
The clouds through the sunny heavens
  As an army walk in white,
On to the gates of glory,
  To the glow of the western light;
So in the snow-white raiment
  That Christ for His child has won,
Thou shalt pass the golden gateway,
  And tell that His work is done.

THE DOOR

ALL within are love and gladness,
  Light and warmth and cheer ;
All without the night wind wailing
  O'er the lonely mere.

There within the child belovèd—
  There the welcome sweet ;
There without the wandering orphan
  And the weary feet.

Wandering child ! the Door is open—
  That fair palace-door ;
There thy Father's kiss awaits thee,
  Fatherless no more.

One fair golden Door—one only,
  Jesus Who has died ;
Jesus is that blessed Doorway
  Open free and wide.

Child, no need to knock, to ask Him
  If thou mayest come ;
Lo ! He stands in love beseeching,
  Saying, " Child ! come home."

Saying, " Child, the night is dreary
    On the mountains lone ;
Pass within thy Father's palace,
    Heaven is all thine own.

Thou hast sinned, and I have suffered
    Curse and death for thee ;
Now as I to Him am precious,
    Thou art dear to Me."

THE MORNING STAR

I woke, and the night was passing,
    And over the hills there shone
A star all alone in its beauty
    When the other stars were gone—

For a glory was filling the heavens
    That came before the day,
And the gloom and the stars together
    Faded and passed away.

Only the star of the morning
  Glowed in the crimson sky—
It was like a clear voice singing,
  " Rejoice! for the Sun is nigh ! "

O children ! a Star is shining
  Into the hearts of men—
It is Christ with a voice of singing,
  " Rejoice ! for I come again !

" For the long, long night is passing,
  And there cometh the golden day ;
I come to My own who love Me,
  To take them all away.

" It may be to-day or to-morrow,
  Soon it will surely be ;
Then past are the tears and the sorrow—
  Then Home for ever with Me."

"WHO PROVIDETH FOR THE RAVEN HIS FOOD?"

ALL the world lay still and silent in the
    morning grey,
And at once a thousand voices hail the
    glorious day;
For the great Sun glowing crimson rises o'er
    the sea—
"Welcome, Day!" they sing together, "Day
    that is to be!"
Oh how glad and sweet and joyous is that
    morning hymn!
Whilst the golden day is stealing through
    the valleys dim—
Thrush and blackbird, lark and linnet, doves
    that coo and hum
Wild delight, and soft rejoicing, for the day
    is come.
Not a thought of care or wonder what the
    day will bring,
For the Father careth for them in the smallest
    thing.

There upon the pathless mountains is their
    table spread,
All by God are known and numbered, by His
    Hands are fed.
Some in deep and tangled forests where the
    berries glow,
Some where children's crumbs are scattered
    on the garden snow,
Some where through the river sedges may-
    flies glance and play,
Some where mountain tarns lie gleaming in
    the hollows grey.
For the wild and hungry eagle, for the wren
    so small,
All is ready—food and gladness, free to each
    and all.

"Ye are of more value than many sparrows.

THE RED, RED SKY.

In the early, early morning, beyond the
    islands green,
Beyond the pines and palm-trees, and the
    purple sea between,

Like the glow through a crimson window
The morning rises slow,
And the isles lie dim in the glory,
And the sea is all aglow.

In the dim and misty evening the purple
    mountains stand,
And the glooms that hush the woodlands lie
    over all the land,
And high in dark-blue heavens the red light
    burns and glows,
Like the jasper of God's city, like the deep
    heart of the rose.
Oh why does morning dawn, and why ends
    the golden day,
With the crimson glow and glory, while
    children kneel and pray ?

Is it thus that God would tell me before the
  day begins
Of the morn of the Day of pardon, the Blood
  that has washed my sins?
The morn of the Day of gladness, the Day of
  His love and grace,
When like the Sun in his glory, the Lord
  unveiled His Face,
And His love shone forth in beauty where
  all was dark before,
For the Blood had been shed which saved
  me, once and for evermore.
Is it thus that God would tell me the evening
  draweth nigh,
When we pass beyond the mountains, beyond
  the purple sky?
And then, in God's great glory the golden
  gates I see,
And sing, "The Blood of Jesus has opened
  them for me!"

MAY DAYS.

God made the sun to give me light,
  The trees to give me shade;
The cowslips and the violets
  For me His Hands have made.

He made the birds to sing to me,
  The blossoms on the tree,
To make me glad in summer days;
  But why did He make me?

O child, how wonderful and sweet
  The answer God has given!
The blessed Lord, who died for thee,
  Has need of thee in Heaven.

To make Him glad in Paradise
  He needs thy little song;
He needs thee for His love and joy
  Where He has waited long.

Oh glad art thou when spring comes in,
  And flowers and birds and bees
Make all the sunny fields rejoice,
  And leaves are on the trees.

O child ! the Lord will have His spring
When these long years are past.
His little ones from every land
Shall be with Him at last.

His lilies and His roses sweet,
His buds and blossoms rare,
All, all His children then shall meet,
And all His joy shall be complete
When they are round Him there.

WHAT SHOULD I SEE?

IF I had the eyes of Heaven,
That could all things see,
Oh what glorious surprises
All around would be !
I should see all still and stately
God's white Angels tread,
Watch me with their eyes of glory,
Sit beside my bed.
When I take the broth to Granny
In her garret mean,
I should see them wait around her,
As around a Queen.

Through the snow in dusky twilight,
    When the winds are wild,
See them speed where lost and lonely
    Strays a little child.
Through the stillness of the noonday
    See them swiftly rise,
Bearing one with face uplighted
    Far into the skies.
Meet them in the lonely places,
    In the busy street,
Ever calm as skies of summer,
    Ever strong and fleet.
Glad and tender in their service,
    For God's love they know
To the smallest and the meanest
    Of His own below.

COWSLIPS.

Long ago, in springs of old,
    Happy days would be,
When in meadows green and gold
    I might wander free.
High the sunny clouds up-piled,
    Blue the April sky,
Birds and flowers and all things wild
    Glad and free as I.
Oh how merry was the shout,
    When the stile was passed,
" Joy! the cowslips all are out!
    Spring is come at last!"
There in sweet and sunny air
    Who can tell the bliss?
Costly shops and gardens fair
    Have no joys like this.
Playthings, countless, fresh, and sweet,
    Scattered wide and free,
All around the children's feet,
    Gifts of God to me.

Whilst I waked, and whilst I slept,
    Through the winter wild,
All the tender flowers He kept
    For His little child—
Kept them safe beneath the snow,
    Safe through wind and rain,
Till in sunshine all aglow
    They arise again.
Oh what joys are kept for me
    In His secret place,
Till the Spring that soon shall be,
    When I see His Face!

A TRUE STORY

ALL alone in the evening grey,
Sick and dying, poor Hannah lay;
Through the broken pane the cold wind
    swept,
Poor Hannah shivered, and moaned, and
    wept.
But it was not cold, and it was not pain,
That made her shiver and moan again :
She did not say, " My pain is sore,"
But " Where shall I be when all is o'er ? "

For Hannah remembered the years gone by,
And she said, " A sinner—a sinner am I !
All black and fearful the sins appear,
That I had forgotten for many a year ;
And thousands, thousands, they come to
mind—
There is hell before and sin behind.
The Lord is holy, and just, and true,
And what He has said He will surely do.
He hath for sin an awful doom,
A lake of fire beyond the tomb ;
And my soul is black with the sins of years,
They cannot be washed away with tears.
And sure it is vain to pray and cry ;
He cannot hear such a sinner as I.
I am going—going—to stand alone,
Before the Lord on His awful throne !"

.　　.　　.　　.　　.

Bright and glad as the stars came out,
With many a laugh and many a shout,
Jack and Will in the garden played,
And they heeded not the noise they made.
But the neighbour calling said, "Children,
dear,
A woman is sick in that house so near ;

There, where the broken pane you see,
She is lying as ill as she can be.
She soon must die, and you see 'tis best
You should be still, and let her rest."
Then in a moment they were still,
For tender hearts had both Jack and Will,
And they sat and looked at the casement
 lone,
Till the stars shone bright, and the day was
 gone.
Then Jack said, "Will, she will go to Heaven,
If she has had her sins forgiven.
I learned at school that when Jesus died
The door of Heaven was opened wide,
Because He was punished Himself for sin.
So now if we die, we can all go in;
Of our sins there will not a word be said,
For Jesus Christ was punished instead;
And if she believes He loves her so,
Beyond the stars her soul will go.
He will lead her in through the golden
 door,
And she will be happy for evermore."
Then Will said, "Jack, that is all quite
 true—
But does she know it as well as you?

What Jesus did we have both been taught,
But some know this, and some do not.
O Jack, maybe she has never known
What it is that the Lord has done ! "
Then Jack said, " If you would help me,
    Will,
I would climb up to the window sill,
And through the hole I would call and say,
' Jesus washes our sins away.' "

.   .   .   .   .

The neighbour said when her work was
    done,
" It may be Hannah is all alone,
And oh ! it's an awful thing to lie
Too ill to live, and afraid to die.
So just to sit with her I will go,
But how to help her I do not know."
So the neighbour went, and she heard no
    moan,
And she thought, " Poor Hannah is dead
    and gone ; "
She lighted the candle with fear and dread,
And stooped to see if Hannah was dead.
But there she lay with her face so bright !
It shone with glory and not with light.

And she said, "O neighbour, the Lord is
　　good !
He has washed me white in His precious
　　Blood,
My sins are gone from before His Face,
And He has prepared a glorious place,
Where those He loves with Himself shall be,
And to that sweet Home He is calling me.
O neighbour, here in the dark I lay,
I felt so guilty I could not pray,
And all my sins like a mountain stood
Before the terrible Face of God.
Then all in a moment, sweet and clear,
A voice spake loud, though none was near,
Like an Angel speaking I heard it say,
'Jesus washes our sins away !'
And whilst I thought, Do my ears tell
　　true ?
It said, ' Poor woman, He died for you.'
And then did the words come sweet and
　　low
That I had forgotten long ago ;
I once heard tell in the years gone by,
How Jesus came on the cross to die,
And there He hung in the darkness dread,
With a crown of thorns on His holy Head.

And some old, old words came back to me,
' He bore our sins on the cursed tree.'
Yes, it was true that mine He bore,
So the guilt is gone, and the judgment
     o'er ;
And more than that, if He died for me,
What must the love of Jesus be !
He in His Home of glory waits
To see me enter the golden gates ;
Whilst I lay moaning in black despair ;
His heart was longing to have me there.
And oh for the welcome I soon shall know !
No words can tell how I long to go ! "

     .   .   .   .   .

And so, ere many a day was done,
There was joy in the Home beyond the sun,
For Hannah had entered the golden door
To dwell with her Saviour for evermore.
God saith that all who to Jesus come
He in His love will welcome home.
The Lord is holy, and just, and true,
And what He hath said, He will surely do.

THE REED

WHEN flowers are red and gold and white,
  And fair is every weed,
The green reeds have no blossom bright—
  I would not be a reed.

For all the summer flowers declare
  In beauty men can see,
How sweet, how glorious, how fair,
  The thoughts of God must be.

Then cut a wandering shepherd boy
  A hollow pipe of reed ;
His little tune of mirth and joy
  Rang far across the mead.

It was the gladness of his heart
  That flowed in music free,
The wild bird has no sweeter art
  That sings upon the tree.

Oh, could I be the little reed,
  To tell afar and near
The joy and love of God above,
  In music sweet and clear !

And all around should hear the sound,
  And know that love Divine
Is not my own, but God's alone,
  His music, and not mine.

Sweet words should cheer the weary ear,
  And tender words the sad,
And none should heed how small the reed ;
  God's love would make them glad.

WINTER AND SUMMER

" The sky is dreary and rainy,
  And the wind makes a restless moan—
And the yellow leaves drift and wander,
  And the songs and the summer are gone.'

Not so, for the gardens are glowing
  In summer beyond the sea,
In the glory of songs and of flowers,
  Whilst here it is winter for thee.

And land after land wakes in sunshine,
  And the grass and the lilies upspring,
And the children shout loud in the meadows,
  And madly the wild birds sing.

K

There is never an end of the summer,
   For round the great world it goes ;
There are somewhere the fields of narcissus,
   And somewhere the sweet red rose.

"Why can I not follow the summer,
   Far over the hills and the sea,
And be always for ever and ever
   Wherever the summer may be ? "

O child, there is summer for ever,
   Here under the wintry sky,
Where the Lord is the light and the glory,
   And His lambs in His pastures lie.

When the snow and the wild sleet are driven
   Far over the lonely mere,
There is summer beyond all the summers,
   Where Jesus the Lord is near.

WATER-LILIES

Who are like the lilies white,
With their crowns all golden bright,
Resting on the waters still,
Underneath the purple hill ?

They are like the saints who stand,
Every one with harp in hand,
On the crystal sea that lies
Far beyond the summer skies.

They are clad in white array,
For their sin is washed away;
Golden crowns for every one,
For they reign beyond the sun,

Over all the Heavens afar,
Over sun and moon and star;
They who low before Him fall,
Reign with Jesus over all.

THE SECRET

Long ago, within a castle
    Far beyond the purple sea,
Dwelt a fair and gracious lady—
    Thus her tale was told to me.

She was like a mystic story
    Of an angel clad in white—
She was like the rest and glory
    Of the starry summer night.

For where sickness was, or sorrow,
 Pain or hunger, want or care,
Bright and sweet and calm and tender,
 Never wearied, she was there.

Unto her the weary-hearted,
 Unto her the sinners came—
She had comfort for their sorrow,
 She had pity for their shame.

And afar in distant countries
 Many a blessèd tale was told,
Of the lady sweet and gracious
 Dwelling in the castle old.

Then went one who longed to comfort
 All the sorrowing and distressed,
There to learn the blessèd secret
 How to give the weary rest.

All day long he watched the lady,
 For he thought that she must pray
Somewhere in a holy chapel
 Surely seven times a day.

But he could not learn the secret,
  Where the lady prayed, or when;
Nor what book of prayers could make her
  Like a well of life to men.

Then another went to watch her—
  Did she fast like hermits old?
Go to services at midnight
  When the winter winds blew cold?

Nay—she ate her food with gladness,
  And at night she only slept;
Rose again refreshed and thankful,
  Fit to comfort those who wept.

Then another went to watch her
  Far across the purple sea;
But her ways were sweet and simple,
  Just as others, so did she.

Yet she seemed attuned to music
  Sounding from a golden chord;
Suddenly he said, "Dear Lady,
  Lovest thou the blessed Lord?"

"Yea," she said, "full well I love Him,
　For I know He loveth me."
Gladly then he sped him homewards
　Far across the purple sea.

IN THE LANES

It is summer all over the meadows,
　All over the woods and the sea ;
How many the glad days of summer
　My Father has given to me !
I think of the long-ago summers,
　With their woodbine and feathery fern—
Of the rambling lanes and the hedgerows—
　Of the tumbling mountain burn.
The foxgloves afar in the forest,
　And the cranesbill soft and blue,
As eyes that look into Heaven
　Till the Heaven itself shines through.
As a story of rapture and wonder
　Are those hedge flowers wild and free,
The travellers' joy and the mullein,
　And the pink thrift near the sea.

The thyme and the marjoram purple,
  The meadow-sweet fair and cool,
Where the reedy streams go wandering
  Down to the deep mill-pool.
The scabious and the yarrow
  Over the chalky down,
The flowering rush in the trenches,
  With rose and crimson crown;
The water violet stately,
  And the frosted bog-bean white
The whole wide world was a marvel,
  A garden of strange delight!
O ye thousand thousand flowers,
  To me as a sign ye stand,
Of the things of joy and wonder
  In the glorious summer land—
The Lord, who has strewn them broadcast
  Over the lonely hills,
Who has filled the woods with music,
  And has gemmed the mountain rills—
Oh what has He made to greet us
  In the land of fair delight,
Where His own shall rejoice before Him,
  And shall walk with Him in white?

ON THE DOWNS

Up the chalky path we wander,
  Higher, higher still—
Gather thyme and hawkweed slender,
  Bluebells of the hill ;
Pale musk mallows by the cornfields,
  Poppies bright and bold,
Scabious like the evening purple,
  Gems amongst the gold.
And the knapweed and the bindweed,
  Yarrow pink and white,
And St. John's wort golden tufted,
  Everywhere delight !
Up the chalky path we wander,
  Higher, higher still,
Now upon the sunny hill-top
  We can rest at will.
Far below the quiet valleys
  Farms and sheep-cotes lie,
All above us deep and cloudless
  Glows the summer sky.
Lying there we look in wonder
  Through the skies afar,

Where unseen to us are shining
Thousand thousand stars.
When the daylight sinks in purple
O'er the silent plain,
One by one, like gathering angels,
They appear again.
Soon, oh soon, the sweet still evening
Of our days will come—
Then will shine the hidden glory
Of our Father's home.
Thousand, thousand radiant faces,
Faces of the past,
Our belovèd, hidden from us,
Smile to us at last.
Wonderful and blessèd evening—
Sudden, sweet surprise—
We shall hear the ancient voices,
See the long-lost eyes.
Here upon the sunny hill-top
Let us thank and praise,
For the blessèd eve that follows
All our summer days.

THE CHILD'S WORK

Oh what can I do for my Lord?
I am foolish, and small, and weak ;
And I know not what to do,
And I know not how to speak.

"O child, there is nought you can do—
Sit down at His Feet and be still ;
But what can He do by you ?
O child, He can do what He will.

He asks for your heart alone,
Then leave to Him all the rest,
For the smallest and weakest one
Is the one He can work with best.

He will work His mighty will
All through the livelong day,
By the child who loves Him well,
Whether at work or play.

His love through your eyes will shine
Till some sad hearts rejoice,
His tenderness move your hands,
Make music in your voice.

His Name will be sweet on your lips,
　As the flowers when the year is young ;
He tells the tale of His love
　The best by a childish tongue.

Where He leads you by the hand,
　The power of God shall go—
A mystery and a might
　As when He walked below.

For Jesus is still the same,
　And He does His marvels still ;
And by His children small
　He works His glorious will.

THE LOST LAMB

LIKE a little wandering lamb
Lost upon the hills I am ;
Like a shepherd Jesus stands,
Holding out His blessed Hands.

"Come," He says, "come back to Me ;
Little lamb, I died for thee ;
I will take thee to My home,
Little lamb, I pray thee come.

"Thou wouldst like to have thy way,
On the lonely hills to stray,
Where the hungry lion hides,
Where the fiery serpent glides.

"I would have thee lie at rest,
Little lamb, upon My breast;
Thou shalt be My sweet delight
All the day and all the night.

"Though thou hast a wayward will,
Little lamb, I love thee still;
Come to Me and be forgiven,
I will bear thee safe to Heaven."

LONG AGO

O LORD JESUS, high in Heaven,
    God's belovèd One,
Crowned with glory and with honour,
    Brighter than the sun—

Art Thou He whom little children
    Knew long years ago,
When a little child amongst them
    Thou didst come and go?

Well they knew the little cottage,
  Small, and poor, and mean,
Where Thou wert a child obedient
  As no child has been—

Holy, true, and tender, doing
  All Thy Father's will ;
If men loved, or if they hated,
  Loving, serving still.

Well they knew the workshop lowly
  Where Thy days were spent,
Through the summer and the winter,
  Peaceful and content.

O Lord Jesus, not as Thou wert
  Have I ever been ;
Selfishness and pride and anger
  In my ways are seen.

Yet I would that I were like Thee,
  Holy, tender, true,
As Thou didst and as Thou spakest
  Would I speak and do.

Never selfish, never murmuring,
Loving, serving all,
Till in heaven amidst Thy glory
At Thy feet I fall—

See Thee who a child became
In a cottage poor,
That I might in Thy fair palace
Dwell for evermore.

THE END.

Printed by BALLANTYNE, HANSON & Co.
Edinburgh & London

FRANCES RIDLEY HAVERGAL.

32mo, 1s. 6d.

UNDER THE SURFACE.
UNDER THE SHADOW.
THE MINISTRY OF SONG.

16mo, 1s.

MY KING.
ROYAL COMMANDMENTS.
ROYAL BOUNTY.
THE ROYAL INVITATION.
LOYAL RESPONSES.
KEPT FOR THE MASTER'S USE.
STARLIGHT THROUGH THE SHADOWS.

32mo, 9d.

MORNING BELLS; or, Waking Thoughts for the Little
Ones. Paper cover, 6d.
LITTLE PILLOWS. Being Good Night Thoughts for the
Little Ones. Paper cover, 6d.
MORNING STARS; or, Names of Christ for His Little
Ones.

MEMORIALS OF FRANCES RIDLEY HAVERGAL. By
her SISTER. Best Edition, 6s. Crown 8vo, 2s. 6d. Cheap
Edition, cloth, 1s. 6d. ; paper covers, 6d.

I

By R. A. TORREY.

PRACTICAL AND PERPLEXING QUESTIONS ANSWERED. Crown 8vo, 1s. 6d.

DIFFICULTIES AND ALLEGED ERRORS AND CONTRADICTIONS IN THE BIBLE. Crown 8vo, 1s. 6d.

ANECDOTES AND ILLUSTRATIONS. Crown 8vo; in cloth, 2s. 6d. *net;* paper covers, 1s. *net.*

HOW TO SUCCEED IN THE CHRISTIAN LIFE. Crown 8vo, 1s. 6d.

WORSHIP. Pott 8vo, 6d.

REAL SALVATION, AND WHOLE-HEARTED SERVICE. Large crown 8vo, 3s. 6d.; in paper covers, 1s. *net.*

TALKS TO MEN ABOUT THE BIBLE AND THE CHRIST OF THE BIBLE. Crown 8vo, 1s. 6d.; in paper covers, 6d. *net.*

REVIVAL ADDRESSES. Large crown 8vo, 3s. 6d.; in paper covers, 1s. *net.*

HOW TO WORK. Demy 8vo, 7s. 6d.
"*A timely production—just the volume for these days of 'united missions, 'great campaigns,' and 'national crusades.' . . . We should like to see it in the hands of every Church member, as well as minister.*"—CHRISTIAN COMMONWEALTH.

THE GIST OF THE LESSONS. Long pott 8vo, Leather, 1s. *net;* in Cloth Limp, 9d. *net.*
"*For the busy teacher . . . the book is most valuable.*"—THE FRIEND.

HOW TO PRAY. Crown 8vo, 1s. 6d.; paper covers, 6d. *net*

THE DIVINE ORIGIN OF THE BIBLE. Cr. 8vo, 1s. 6d.
"*The pages are impressive in fact and strong in argument—such a book was wanted.*"—THE CHRISTIAN.

WHAT THE BIBLE TEACHES. Demy 8vo, 7s. 6d.
"*A really remarkable book. The very simplicity of the method helping to a clear understanding of the doctrine treated.*"—THE RECORD.

HOW TO OBTAIN FULNESS OF POWER. Cr. 8vo, 1s. 6d.

HOW TO BRING MEN TO CHRIST. Crown 8vo, 1s. 6d.; paper covers, 6d. *net.*

HOW TO STUDY THE BIBLE FOR GREATEST PROFIT. Crown 8vo, 1s. 6d.
"*Every word tells and conveys precious facts of persistent Bible research . . we warmly commend this admirable little compendium.*"—SWORD AND TROWEL.

THE BAPTISM WITH THE HOLY SPIRIT. Cr. 8vo, 1s.
"*Helpful to all who desire to make their Christian discipleship a reality.*"—THE CHRISTIAN CHURCH.

THE VEST POCKET COMPANION FOR CHRISTIAN WORKERS. Leather, 1s. *net.*
"*A capital little book for workers.*"—THE ROCK.

By FRANCES A. BEVAN.

THE EARNEST OF THE SPIRIT. Crown 8vo, 1s.

COME! Gospel Hymns. Crown 8vo, 1s. 6d.

HYMNS OF TER STEEGEN, SUSO, AND OTHERS.
FIRST SERIES. Crown 8vo, 1s. 6d.

"The literary quality of many of the hymns will be welcome to many lovers of sacred poetry."—*Manchester Guardian.*

"The versification is good, and many of the hymns are worthy of a recognised place in English Hymnology."—*Aberdeen Free Press.*

HYMNS OF TER STEEGEN AND OTHERS. SECOND
SERIES. Crown 8vo, 1s. 6d.

"A volume of very choice pieces."—*The Christian.*

"Choicely printed volume, sure to be prized highly as a gift book . . . remarkable for sweetness and the strength of its sober exaltation."—*Yorkshire Post.*

TREES PLANTED BY THE RIVER. Crown 8vo, 4s. 6d.

"This excellent book will commend itself to many a contemplative Christian during hours of quiet communion with his own soul and with God."—*Christian Commonwealth.*

"A deeply interesting book."—*Aberdeen Free Press.*

THREE FRIENDS OF GOD. Records from the Lives of
JOHN TAULER, NICHOLAS OF BASLE, HENRY SUSO. Crown 8vo, 2s. 6d.

"Fascinating glimpses of the strange religious life of mediæval Europe. No student of history and human nature can fail to be interested by this book, while to pious minds it will bring stimulus and edification."—*Scotsman.*

"The simplicity and austerity of life of these great men are depicted with graphic and sympathetic touch."—*Court Journal.*

3

L

By the Rev. J. REID HOWATT.

THE CHILDREN'S PREACHER. A Year's Addresses
and Parables for the Young. Crown 8vo, 2s. 6d.

THE CHILDREN'S PEW. Sermons to Children. Crown
8vo, 2s. 6d.

THE CHILDREN'S PULPIT. A Year's Sermons and
Parables for the Young. Crown 8vo, 2s. 6d.

THE CHILDREN'S ANGEL. Being a Volume of Sermons
to Children. Crown 8vo, 2s. 6d.

YOUTH'S IDEALS. Small crown 8vo, 1s.

"So bright and cheerful, so clever and well written, yet so full of deep
Christian earnestness, that we would like to see it circulated by tens of
thousands."—*The New Age.*

AFTER HOURS ; or, The Religion of Our Leisure Time.
With Appendix on How to Form a Library for Twenty Shillings.
Small crown 8vo, 1s.

THE CHILDREN'S PRAYER BOOK : Devotions for the
Use of the Young for One Month. Cloth extra, pott 8vo, 1s.

LIFE WITH A PURPOSE. A Book for Girls and Young
Men. Small crown 8vo, 1s.

4

THE BIBLICAL LIBRARY.

A Series of Volumes on Biblical Subjects written by able and well-known scholars, and designed so that, whilst helpful to the student, they will be of great interest to the general reader. Full crown 8vo, 3s. 6d. each.

VOL. I.

THE HERODS. By the Very Rev. F. W. FARRAR, D.D., F.R.S., Dean of Canterbury.

VOL. II.

WOMEN OF THE OLD TESTAMENT: STUDIES IN WOMANHOOD. By the Rev. R. F. HORTON, M.A., D.D.

VOL. III.

THE HISTORY OF EARLY CHRISTIANITY. By Rev. LEIGHTON PULLAN, of Oxford University.

VOL. IV.

WOMEN OF THE NEW TESTAMENT. By Rev. Professor W. F. ADENEY.

VOL. V.

THE FAITH OF CENTURIES. By the BISHOP OF ROCHESTER, the BISHOP OF CALCUTTA, Bishop BARRY, Canon SCOTT HOLLAND, Professor RYLE, and others.

By the Rev. GEORGE MATHESON, D.D.

TIMES OF RETIREMENT. A Volume of Devotional Readings. Crown 8vo, 2s. 6d.

MOMENTS ON THE MOUNT. A Series of Devotional Meditations. Crown 8vo, 2s. 6d.

VOICES OF THE SPIRIT. Crown 8vo, 2s. 6d.

By the Rev. JAMES WELLS, M.A.

BIBLE OBJECT LESSONS. Addresses to Children. With Illustrations. Crown 8vo, 2s. 6d.

BIBLE ECHOES. Addresses to the Young. Crown 8vo, 2s. 6d.

THE PARABLES OF JESUS. Crown 8vo, 2s. 6d.

5

By the Rev. A. T. PIERSON, D.D.

THE BIBLE AND SPIRITUAL LIFE. Large crown 8vo, 5s. *net.*

THE BIBLE AND SPIRITUAL CRITICISM. Large crown 8vo, 3s. 6d. *net.*

GOD'S LIVING ORACLES. Large crown 8vo, 3s. 6d. *net.*

THE MODERN MISSION CENTURY. A Review of the Missions of the Nineteenth Century with Reference to the Superintending Providence of God. Large crown 8vo, 6s.

JAMES WRIGHT OF BRISTOL. A Memorial of a Fragrant Life. Illustrated. Large crown 8vo, 3s. 6d. *net.*

GEORGE MÜLLER OF BRISTOL. With 13 full-page illustrations. Crown 8vo, 2s. 6d. *net.*

THE NEW ACTS OF THE APOSTLES. Being Lectures on Foreign Missions delivered under the Duff Endowment. With Coloured Chart, showing the Religions of the World and the Progress of Evangelisation. Extra crown 8vo, 3s. 6d. *net.*

"As a repertory of missionary facts and arguments, this work is as deeply interesting as the style is truly enthusiastic, and we bespeak for it a wide circle of readers, whom it will assuredly stimulate to increased zeal in sending the Gospel throughout the world."—*Christian.*

"Such a work as this ought greatly to help in the evangelisation of the whole world."—*Sword and Trowel.*

"Emphatically the handbook of Missions."—*Presbyterian.*

By FREDERICK A. ATKINS.

ASPIRATION AND ACHIEVEMENT. A Young Man's Message to Young Men. Small crown 8vo, 1s.

Dr. R. F. HORTON writes: "I have rarely read a more salutary book."

MORAL MUSCLE: AND HOW TO USE IT. A Brotherly Chat with Young Men. By F. A. ATKINS, Editor of "The Young Man." With an Introduction by Rev. THAIN DAVIDSON, D.D. Small crown 8vo, 1s.

Dr. CLIFFORD writes: "It is full of life, throbs with energy, is rich in stimulus, and bright with hope."

FIRST BATTLES, AND HOW TO FIGHT THEM. By F. A. ATKINS, Editor of "The Young Man." Small crown 8vo, 1s.

"Another of Mr. Atkins' capital little books for young men."— *British Weekly.*

6